DEATH MARCH

By now the searching soldiers had seen him. They pointed and conferred. Two hurried toward him.

"You all right?" asked one.

Noel's courage returned. If they could see him and he could hear them, then perhaps his position had finally stabilized. He dared to take a step toward them and didn't dematerialize . . .

The ground was rough and uneven. Noel stumbled, and one of the soldiers gripped his arm in support.

"Thanks," said Noel. "I'm kind of—"

His voice died in his throat. He stared at the man's hand on his sleeve. Where there should have been a normal appendage with flesh, skin, and hair, there was only a skeleton. Fingers of polished bone gleamed white in the gathering gloom . . .

Ace Books by Sean Dalton

The Time ∞ Trap Series

TIME ∞ TRAP
SHOWDOWN
PIECES OF EIGHT
RESTORATION
TURNCOAT

Operation Starhawks Series

SPACE HAWKS
CODE NAME PEREGRINE
BEYOND THE VOID
THE ROSTMA LURE
DESTINATION: MUTINY
THE SALUKAN GAMBIT

CHAPTER 1

Noel Kedran ran for his life down a sloping hill, his feet sinking ankle-deep in snow, his coattails flying behind him. Around him came the furious rattle of musket fire, sounding like hailstones on a sheet of tin.

As he ran, his feet slipping and sliding on the icy ground, he was filled with fury and bewilderment. What was he doing here? He'd accomplished his mission in seventeenth-century England. He thought he'd done everything right. Recall through the time stream should have returned him to the Time Institute. Instead he was in the wrong century and the wrong location, running like a scared rabbit in the middle of a pitched battle.

So what had gone wrong?

There was no time to wonder, no time to go through the routine self-check following travel. He'd scarcely materialized and reoriented himself in the reality of this dimension before the battle that was raging on these hillsides came his way.

A lead musket ball whined past his head, and Noel ducked lower. His feet slipped out from under him. Arms windmilling, he fell with enough force to numb his backside forever, and slid down a ditch into a thicket of briars and bushes.

Scrambling desperately for cover beneath a thorny bush that lacked a single concealing leaf, Noel flattened himself to the ground behind a fallen log and tried to catch his breath. Beneath the snow, the ground was a sodden layer of rotted leaf mulch. Some kind of small animal had made a den for itself in the end of the old log. Noel could smell the pungent odors. Briars had caught in the back of his coat. Each time he shifted a fraction, he could hear tiny rips in the cloth. He felt exposed and vulnerable in this all but useless hiding place. Anyone on the hill above him could probably see him if they bothered to look.

Only there, in that moment of hiding, did he have his first chance to take stock of the situation.

Something was wrong.

Even as the thought crossed his mind, he dismissed it impatiently. Of course something was wrong. He'd landed in the wrong century again.

But it was more than that. He stared up the hill, his breath fogging from his nostrils, and found the perspective slightly off-kilter. It was like looking at a picture shot through an elongated lens. The sky seemed to curve too sharply toward the earth.

Distortion, he thought in dismay and realized the time stream's anomaly had not been corrected.

As long as he moved quickly and did not look at any object too long, all appeared normal enough. But stop and remain motionless, as he was doing now in his hiding place, and the shapes around him began to take on a surreal quality. It was Kroginer's Effect, which said that an object displaced to an alternate dimension must travel roughly forty-seven times cubed the velocity of objects within said dimension in order to intercept the discontinuity curve for positive entry. Failure to achieve this velocity would result in a distortion curve at exponential rates, nullifying entry or generating an anomaly proportionate to—

To the thunderous pounding of drums, a contingent of soldiers in scarlet coats appeared over the crest of the hill he'd just come down. Marching in a precise line, they looked grim indeed in their bright uniforms and tall, peaked hats. They carried Brown Betsy muskets with bayonets affixed, deadly weapons for the day. At the bawled command of an officer, the men knelt, aimed their muskets, and fired.

Musket balls whizzed over the thicket where Noel was hiding. While he knew he wasn't their target, he still pressed his face to the ground and prayed for accurate shooting. *Caught in the crossfire* wasn't the kind of epithet he wanted. Especially since he wasn't supposed to be anywhere near the American Revolution of the late eighteenth century.

It had to be another closed time loop, another trap. Once before he'd been caught in a time stream from which there was no return. Escaping that had nearly killed him and he'd sworn never to return to the past. At least until circumstances had dragged him back. Now, he closed his fists on the snow until they shook and ice melted against his palms. His sacrifice, risking a dangerous return to the past to close the anomaly, had been for nothing.

But right now wasn't a good time to rage against the malfunction that had brought him here. Noel figured he'd better save his skin first and worry about the future later. He'd inadvertently materialized in the middle of a battlefield, and all he wanted to do was scramble clear before someone shot him by mistake.

The British were still firing in wonderful precision, the front line kneeling to reload while the second line fired, then all advancing a few feet, only to start the entire process again. From the American side came a return volley of fire, ragged and random. Men screamed in death, and the acrid smoke of burnt gunpowder boiled across the frozen land.

In the distance Noel could hear screams and battle cries mingled with the terrifying whistle of cannonballs and the steady beat of drums. He'd managed to skirt the main battlefield, only to run into this smaller skirmish between the redcoats and the patriots. The latter took cover guerrilla style and confined themselves to potshots. The soldiers in scarlet kept to formation despite the appalling cost of lives. It seemed to Noel, caught in the crossfire, that the colonials were retreating because they constantly shifted their position. But whether they were actually trying to flee or were leading the British soldiers into a trap, he didn't know.

All he was sure of was that he didn't want to remain caught between the two forces.

Without warning the world went black and soundless for at least eight seconds. It was as though the entire universe had suddenly paused.

I'm hit, thought Noel in a fleeting moment of panic.

But he was not injured. He was in the nowhere of between, that eerie, formless place of no dimension. What had suddenly swept him here, he could not determine.

Light returned, blinding him at first, then reality resumed. Only, what had happened to the hillside, the snow, the ditch where he'd been hiding? Too astonished to comprehend what had happened, Noel turned around in a small circle.

He stood on flat ground, the grass brown under his feet, autumn leaves in bright hues of scarlet and gold fluttering in the wind. Dense fog surrounded him, so gray and impenetrable that it looked like cotton wool. The sounds of battle crashed on nearby—muffled by the fog. Noel heard hoofbeats approaching and ran awkwardly toward the dimly seen trees. The ground was soft from rain. The air smelled of smoke and damp. Musket fire rattled away, then a contingent of horsemen galloped by like ghosts in the enveloping mists. Noel heard the wail of a bugle and the answering shouts of men.

He reached the woods, blundering against the wet, reassuring roughness of a tree trunk. His palm scraped over the bark . . . and the world shifted and went black again.

This shift was not as long as the previous one—a split second in duration, no longer than a blink. Yet it took Noel some time to assimilate it.

Back in the ditch in the snow beneath the bush. The fog was gone. Sunshine glittered coldly off the snow. Shouts and the sound of running feet gave him little warning before a small squadron of redcoats came trampling through the ditch where he was hiding. Noel tensed in wild alarm. Where had they come from?

He had no time to run, no time to think. Weaponless, he hadn't a prayer of protecting himself.

Noel popped up like a rabbit and held his hands high in surrender.

He found himself face-to-face with a man in a white wig and pointed hat. The soldier's face was bloodstained and twisted in a violent grimace. His eyes were wild with battle madness. At the sight of Noel, he didn't check but came on with a vicious thrust of his bayonet.

"Hey!" said Noel but there was no time to protest. He dodged to one side, and felt the bayonet slice through the side of his coat, close enough for him to feel cold metal. Noel's heart jumped, and he thought he would be sick. This was no distortion shift; this was reality.

"Wait!" he said. "I'm a civilian. I'm not a part of this—"

"Damned colonial traitors!" shouted another soldier. "Stick 'im quick, Polk, before 'e shoots you in the back."

The bayonet came at Noel again, aiming at his midsection. Noel jumped back, stumbled, and nearly fell against another soldier. They were all around him now. Gore dripped from the tips of their bayonets. The stench of blood, sweat, and gunsmoke reeked in their uniforms. He had nothing with which to defend himself, not a dagger, not a pistol—all his weapons had vanished during his journey through the time stream.

God help me, Noel thought. *What am I doing here?*

"I surrender!" he said in open desperation. "I'm your prisoner."

They grinned like wolves. And more redcoats were coming over the hill.

"I surrender," he said, gulping for breath. "I claim clemency under the rules of civilized warfare."

The soldier holding him at bay laughed. Noel looked into his blue eyes and saw only contempt and no mercy at all. It made his blood run cold.

Just before the soldier struck at him, Noel twisted and grabbed at another man's arm, seeking to wrest away the pistol tucked in his belt. He was shook off and went sprawling on the slippery ground. A bayonet plunged into the mud a scant inch from his face. Noel rolled frantically and scrambled to his feet, despite a shove that nearly knocked him down again.

Shift! he prayed desperately. If time was not stable, then let it yank him out of here.

The soldiers circled him like wolves. How they could take the time to play this deadly cat-and-mouse game in the middle of an attack was beyond him. All he knew was he had to defend himself somehow until the next shift or die. Yet what if one of them tired of the game and simply shot him?

He faced his principal attacker again, breathing hard. His only advantage lay in the narrowness of the ditch. There was little room to maneuver, and the soldiers had to be careful not to impale each other. One man feinted at Noel, and when he tried to elude it, another stabbed at him. Noel dropped to the ground between the men, and once again both blades missed him.

"Devil take the bloke!" shouted one in exasperation.

"Men, forward!" came a shout.

Still panting on the ground, Noel thought the command was his salvation. They had to keep advancing. No more time for games. Noel lifted his head and looked into the soldier's eyes.

The man simply raised his musket and fired.

A belch of white smoke, deafening noise, and the ball crashed into Noel's temple. For an instant he saw nothing but blinding white light. Then all was a gummy, swimming darkness while their feet trampled over him to the next fray.

CHAPTER 2

Reality shift:
DATA . . . *Subject One undergoing altered dimensional state. Molecular shift. No directional path on time stream. Intrusion likely.*

DATA . . . *Subject Two exiting from time stream. Directional path on course. No intrusion.*

DATA . . . *Subject One now between dimensions. No directional path on time stream. Intrusion imminent.*

DATA . . . *Subject Two gone from time stream. Entry point two spatial points from Subject One's initial entry and exit.*

DATA . . . *Subject One intruding. Termination advised.*

INSTRUCTIONS . . . *Qwip activation.*

CHAPTER 3

Silence floated over the world, blessed quietness after the raging chaos of the day. In the hedgerow a bird whistled, soft and tentative, as though wondering whether it was safe to return. Noel knelt upon the trampled earth, his heart racing, his nerve endings still tingling from the suddenness of his transference to this place. His wits felt scattered, as though half of them had been left behind on that snowy battlefield, where he should have died.

The redcoat had shot him point-blank, sending him spinning back into infinity. Now he had materialized here, whole and safe but confused. He staggered to his feet, utterly disoriented, and tried to make sense of what had happened.

The land around him was sheathed in fog, so thick and white he could almost scoop it into his hand. Overhead, the sky held dirty, gray clouds, and the gloom was so deep he could not judge what hour of day it was. The trees beyond this clearing where he stood had leaves ablaze in autumn glory.

Noel rubbed the condensing moisture from his face. Moments before he'd been in deep snow. He'd gone from winter to autumn. Was he moving backward through time, or forward? And why was he skipping from materialization to materialization like this?

"LOC," he said.

There came the sound of approaching hoofbeats splashing over the sodden ground.

"Cancel," said Noel.

Glancing around, he ran for cover.

With the first step he took, however, the world fuzzed and vanished around him into a kaleidoscope of broken shapes and colors. He spun back and tried to retreat, but the fragments twirled around him, cutting him off from reality. Scarlet he saw, and blue. Yellow cut across violet, and multiple hues of green cartwheeled crazily. He flung out his hands in an instinctive effort to hold the shapes away from him.

"No!" he shouted.

An invisible force knocked him down. He thought the ground no longer existed and expected to fall through infinity, but instead he hit solid earth with a grunt of pain.

In a twinkling, the abstract shapes of color disappeared, and a recognizable world surrounded him again. The fog, however, had vanished, to be replaced by indigo twilight stretching forth from the trees. Figures moved here and there in the gloom. Clad in late eighteenth-century uniforms and carrying muskets, they appeared to be searching. The air stank of death, and crows shrieked from the treetops in anticipation of carrion.

Noel staggered to his feet, feeling shaken and bruised. His head was throbbing, and he felt close to nausea. Nearby lay the mangled body of a man killed by a cannonball. Noel stared a moment, then turned away and was sick.

Clammy and aching, he straightened and wiped his mouth. He was afraid to move, afraid he would be cast between dimensions again. He hadn't traveled through the time portal into his own century, but it was becoming obvious that he was out of sync with this era. His Light Operated Computer must be trying to stabilize his coordinates, but he kept fading in and out, kept shifting to various times within this general location grid.

Something was holding him to the Revolutionary War.

He didn't have to guess too hard to know what it was.

Leon.

His worst nightmare. His enemy. A piece of himself. He sighed, weary of the struggle that never ended.

By now the searching soldiers had seen him. They pointed and conferred. Two hurried toward him.

"You all right?" asked one.

Noel's courage returned. If they could see him and he could

hear them, then perhaps his position had finally stabilized. He dared to take a step toward them and didn't dematerialize.

He grinned to himself in relief and took another step. His knees were wobbly, but that didn't matter. His headache didn't matter. Right now all he wanted was for the world to stay solid until he could figure out what to do. Lengthening his stride, he walked toward the men.

The ground was rough and uneven. Noel stumbled, and one of the soldiers gripped his arm in support.

"Thanks," said Noel. "I'm kind of—"

His voice died in his throat. He stared at the man's hand on his sleeve. Where there should have been a normal appendage with flesh, skin, and hair, there was only a skeleton. Fingers of polished bone gleamed white in the gathering gloom. They tightened around his biceps, then loosened. Noel tried to swallow and couldn't. He forced himself to look up into the man's face. Beneath the tricorn hat and old-fashioned clothes, there was only a skeleton. Empty sockets stared at him from the skull. Bony metacarpals curled around the musket, and a woolen muffler dangled absurdly around the vertebrae of the thing's neck.

All the blood seemed to drain from Noel's head. He felt suddenly dizzy and lost. Animated skeletons? Trying to come to grips with the situation, he stepped back and glanced across the battlefield. Pale forms were rising from the dead bodies, some hovering as though reluctant to leave, others zipping away.

"No," said Noel hoarsely. "I do not believe this."

"Shocked out of himself," said the one skeletal soldier to its companion.

"He's making no sense to me," agreed the other. "Better walk him along."

"Aye."

Noel whirled around to fend them off, and found himself facing two young men who were hardly more than boys. Their faces were grimed, blood-splattered, and stubbled with beard growth. One wore his hair tied back in a queue; the other's was unbound and stringy. Noel stared in fresh astonishment. What *was* this? Either he was experiencing time distortions or he wasn't. Either he was out of sync or he wasn't. Maybe he was just going crazy.

His head went round and round; perhaps for an instant he fainted. A sturdy shoulder went beneath his arm, and he found himself supported by a strong arm.

He shuddered, but the man assisting him was no walking skeleton.

"Come on," muttered the man. "You're heavier than you look."

Noel stumbled along, his senses swimming, his mind awash with confused questions. As his vision cleared, he glanced back at the battlefield, half-fearing to see more ghosts rising from the bodies. But all he saw were the searchers moving from form to form, trying to sort the living from the dead.

A bridle jingled. A horse and rider were approaching. The man supporting Noel muttered beneath his breath and straightened, juggling Noel enough to free one arm for a salute.

The horse drew up and stopped, snorting. Noel squinted through the twilight. Silhouetted against the inky sky sat a tall man with a heavy, expressionless face. He was wrapped in a dark blue cloak, and wore a tricorne hat pulled low to protect him from the frosty cold. Condensed air blew from the nostrils of his gray horse.

Ghost horse? wondered Noel.

He recognized the rider, whose face he'd known since his earliest school days.

"Washington," he whispered.

The soldier holding him gave him a dig in the ribs. "That's General Washington to the likes of you!"

"Gently, Sergeant, gently," admonished the general. "Put him in the ranks of walking wounded."

"Yes, sir."

The sergeant saluted again, and Washington rode on, followed by his dejected officers and adjutants. Noel stared after them, his historian's soul touched to the core by this encounter.

"Walking wounded," muttered the sergeant. "Walking disaster is more like it. The name of Germantown will hang over our heads in shame for the rest of our lives, not that we're likely to have them much longer, what with the way this bloody war is going. Come on, come on, move your feet, you!"

He shuffled Noel forward to the band of silent soldiers. Many sported such terrible wounds Noel could not believe they were able to stand up, much less walk. Their makeshift bandages were less than adequate. The night air was growing very cold indeed and few men wore a complete uniform. Some were in civilian clothing, like Noel. Others were walking bundles of rags.

No wonder, he thought, then couldn't remember the rest of what he'd been thinking.

He sagged, but the sergeant hoisted him up again and thrust

him at a gaunt fellow with an arm in a sling.

"Here, you! Got one good arm left, don't you? Use it to help your mate. Line! Keep moving!"

They stumbled forward. There was no talking, no jokes, no grumbling. Noel pulled himself together, trying to walk steadily although his legs remained weak. His pride gouged him. These men had serious injuries; all he suffered from was a little distortion sickness. He had to do at least as well as they. Germantown, he thought, longing to access his LOC for information. Germantown had been an important battle. Pennsylvania? Close to Philadelphia? They'd lost, badly, from the looks of things. Why they weren't prisoners Noel had no idea. His specialty was not American history. But wasn't this defeat the last major battle Washington attempted before withdrawing to Valley Forge?

An involuntary shiver that had nothing to do with the cold air ran along Noel's spine.

He glanced at his companion and again found himself in the company of a walking skeleton. The bandage covering half of the man's face was now swathed over a bare skull. A bony arm rested in the bloodied sling. Through the trees other skeletons walked with them in grim silence, punctuated now and then by a low moan. The hairs stood up on the back of Noel's neck. He wanted to break away, to run, but he hadn't the strength.

Maybe he was just hallucinating, he told himself. Skeletons didn't walk. They didn't wear clothes and bandages. They didn't carry muskets. He decided this distortion sickness was playing games with his mind.

Twilight darkened to night. The chilly wind died down, and in the woods surrounding them there lay an unnatural hush. Stumbling over uneven ground, his cheek smarting from where limbs had whipped it, Noel drew in a ragged breath and then another as he struggled to keep his sanity.

I will close my eyes, and these creatures will return to their normal appearance, he told himself. *I am not really walking with the dead.*

"Are we going to Valley Forge?" he forced himself to ask.

"Where?" replied his companion. "Never heard of it."

"Quiet!" said the skeleton ahead of them, twisting its skull around to glare at Noel with empty sockets. "No talking."

"Damned old Howe," muttered Noel's companion. "I hope he rots this winter. I hope he gets food poisoning at one of them fancy parties thrown in his honor by the fine citizens of Philadelphia. I hope he gets gout and they have to cut his foot off."

"It's cannonballs what takes off yer foot," whispered the man behind Noel, "not gout."

"Shush!" said someone else.

And they were men again, their faces restored, their breath fogging from their nostrils. They walked with pain and courage, afraid to linger behind and be captured, following a general they loved into the unknown of the darkness.

They did not stop to rest. They found no shelter, although more than once they crept past snug farmsteads, where golden light shone from the windows and cattle lowed within the barns. There was no medical assistance, no food, no fire. Noel's fingers and toes grew numb. He ceased to be aware of his body as it lurched and struggled, yet somehow he kept going.

If he slept at all during that long, horrible night of marching, he did so in snatches of unconsciousness caught between one footstep and the next. His sense of disorientation grew, although the hallucinations did not return. His brain felt disjointed, if an organ without joints could be in such a condition. But even his wandering wits found no answers to the half-formed questions that worried him.

He had stopped shifting, but was he now in a stable location? Would he shift again? Would the hallucinations grow worse? If he tried to travel again, where would the distortion field throw him? Had the future been wiped out by now? Had he failed? What should he do next?

He tried to reason out a plan and was unable to concentrate long enough to form one. He tried to keep going, but he couldn't.

He fell to his knees, dragging his companion halfway down with him.

The man tugged at him. "Get up! You want to be shot?"

Noel coughed violently. His chest ached from the cold air he was breathing. What had happened to climate control? he wondered. Who had let drizzle fall at this hour? The shuttle traffic across Lake Michigan was going to be snarled up forever. He'd be late for work again, and Rugle would slap more demerits on his record. The old hag didn't allow excuses.

"Institute," he said aloud.

His mind cleared momentarily. He remembered his training, his coworkers, his friends, and those he disliked. He realized he needed to break away from this army and access his LOC. As long as the distortions were happening, the time stream was still active. That meant he had a slight chance to get back before . . .

"Come on. Get up!"

Dragged to his feet, Noel staggered forward. His headache returned, driving away memory and clarity. Frustrated, he grimaced against the pain pounding through his left temple. What had he been trying to remember? What was he going to do? There was urgency, yet how could he act if he didn't understand?

The more he walked the worse he felt. He began to hear bones rattling together around him. He shivered, trying to draw away from his companion. The more he moved about, the greater the distortion effect. That meant he should remain still.

Noel stumbled to a halt.

The skeleton at his side tugged at him. "Come on."

"I'm not going."

"You will, or you'll die."

"I'm not going." Already his headache was lessening. His mind grew sharper in the relief. He turned aside but took no step.

"Deserters are shot."

The men staggered around them, parting like a stream around a rock. One was whimpering. Another whispered prayers to himself.

"Don't you care about anything 'sides yourself?" asked Noel's companion angrily. "Hell, you ain't even bleeding and already you want to go home. That's the trouble with you militia. No sense of discipline. No sense of being an army. Go ahead and desert us, then. We don't need any yellow-livered belly crawlers like you."

Noel drew breath, but a sound was whispering down the line, passed along like hope from one man to the next.

"Halt."

"Halt the line."

The soldiers stopped and stood like dumb cattle. Some of them sagged down with groans. Officers on horseback rode by, checking and questioning. Others walked among the men, voices quiet and low, approaching, pausing, moving on. Lantern light flickered fairy quick, was shuttered, then appeared again.

Noel crouched against a tree trunk, drawing in deep breaths, hoping to be forgotten in the darkness. Staying still was his only hope.

Lantern light blinded him. "This man lacks a cloak," said a voice.

Someone moved between him and the light to drape a blanket

over his shoulders. Hands probed at him, checking for injuries.

"Nothing wrong here but exhaustion."

"Not a wagon candidate," said the voice behind the lantern. "He'll do. Feed him."

The footsteps went to the next man. Noel didn't bother to watch them. He was afraid he'd see one skeleton ministering to another. A shadow approached him through the darkness and a measure of water was pressed to his lips. He gasped at how cold it was, then drank thirstily.

The shadow pressed something round and fist-sized into his hand. "Eat it sharp now. Sorry it ain't hot, but it's the best we got."

"Coffee?" asked the next man.

The shadow moved away from Noel. "Sorry, there's no coffee tonight. Just water."

"Hell! How're we to march without nothing to warm our bellies?"

Noel tuned out the argument and turned the object around in his fingers. It had the shape and heft of an irregular-shaped ball. He sniffed it, and it smelled earthy. He bit into it cautiously and discovered it was a raw turnip.

He nearly spat it out.

But it was food, and he was hungry. He forced himself to eat the unpleasant thing.

By the time he finished choking it down, his mouth was puckered from the taste, and his stomach ached in protest. The order was passed for the men to go on.

Noel pressed himself deeper into the shadows, pulling the blanket over his face to keep his skin from gleaming in any stray beam of lantern light. He crouched there, listening to them pass, struggling, biting back sounds of pain. His heart went out to them, but he was not part of their history. He could not help them. He dared not join them.

At long last they were gone. He waited still longer, until his muscles grew cramped and tired and his impatience could not be contained. Pulling down the blanket, he listened for any sounds of marching. All was silent.

Shivering, he said, "LOC, activate."

He felt the slightest pulse of response from his computer, then there came a weird blaze of light overhead as though the sun had suddenly risen. The darkness flowed back, fleeing a rosy gold illumination that spread across the treetops. Dazzled by it, Noel squinted and looked around.

The land looked bloody in the pinkish light. The trees began to shrink as though a fold had appeared in the earth itself and all things were being drawn into it.

"LOC!" said Noel in alarm. "Activate now. Initiate—"

He never finished his sentence. There was a surge of blackness through his head, and the strange pink light vanished. The whole world vanished, and he fell into the blackness as though he had never been.

CHAPTER 4

Reality shift:

Weightlessness . . . formlessness . . . Noel drifted in small eddies of nowhere, lost in the moist darkness of sound and shape without meaning.

His thoughts eventually took cohesion. His brain called forth memories of the original time anomaly, when shifts and rips had threatened to destroy the Institute. Then he had been caught in the nightmare, a part of it, a cause of it, until time itself reached into reality for him and flung him back into the past.

Now it was happening again . . .

"No."

The voice startled him. He tried to look around, but he was still floating in darkness, lacking reference point, lacking body.

"Leon?" he asked uncertainly.

"No."

That flat reply startled him. How could anyone else be here between dimensions? It was a physical law that two travelers could not enter the time stream at the same time. Two travelers could not visit the same coordinates in the past at the same time. What, then, had happened to change physics?

"Who?" he asked in bewilderment.

"What."

Noel hesitated, trying to understand this odd communication.

"I am what," said the voice impatiently.

Still Noel did not understand. Lacking reference points, his wits seemed to be gone too. "You are what," he said stupidly. "I don't understand."

"TERMINATION RECOMMENDED," boomed over him.

Noel cringed, his consciousness bobbing in the eddies and currents of nondimension.

"Focus," said the voice curtly to him. "You seek reference. You ask who in an effort at identification. *What* is more precise."

Noel frowned. This voice sounded like a computer. "LOC?" he asked with caution.

"Your crude device is not operational in these coordinates."

"I still don't understand. What has happened to me? Why am I back between dimensions?"

"TERMINATION RECOMMENDED," boomed again.

Rattled by it, Noel cried out, "What is that?"

"Termination."

"Termina—You mean *death*?"

"Communication has failed," said the voice with a sigh. "Accede to recommenda—"

"Wait!" said Noel. "Why am I to be terminated? What have I done?"

"Violation of our dimension is not permitted."

"Vio—" Noel cut himself off and thought hard. "You mean, you're from another—"

"You have entered an alternate dimension. Your technology is limited, but you should be cognitive of the theory."

"Yes, of course," said Noel. His mind reeled at the implications. It seemed he had made contact across time. Not *down* the time stream, not *along* the time stream, but *across* the time stream. Alternate dimensions, parallel universes. Perhaps he was talking to himself from another—

"No," said the voice. "Do not speculate about matters you cannot comprehend."

"You're telepathic?" asked Noel. He was beginning to recover from his initial shock. His powers of observation, limited though they were by being able to see and feel nothing, stretched acutely.

"Explanations are beyond your limited abilities to comprehend."

"Aw, come on," said Noel, goaded. "Try to say it in simple terms. I bet I could get at least some of it."

"TERMINATION RECOMMENDED."

That pronouncement seemed louder and more forceful than ever. Angry, Noel said, "Can't you turn that off? I don't want to be terminated. If I've done something wrong or trespassed somehow, I apologize. We've been having some trouble with rips in time."

"Anomalies," said the voice.

"Yeah. It has to do with—"

"Explanations are not necessary. We have monitored this intrusion."

Noel blinked, thinking about another dimension aware of his. Possibly even watching his. It was a chilling thought.

"I've been trying to repair it," he said. "It's been messing up my, uh, dimension. I guess it's played some havoc with yours."

"Yes."

"Sorry," said Noel. "It's a long story, but due to sabotage I was trapped in the past, uh, my past—"

"Dimensions do not cross," broke in the voice impatiently. "Awkward delineations are not necessary."

"Right. Anyway, I was trapped. While I was in the time stream, something else went wrong and I was duplicated. Later on, when my people rescued me, we somehow left the duplicate behind. That separation caused the anomaly. I traveled back to get him, but I guess I failed. I should have returned to the Institute by now. Instead . . ." Noel's voice trailed off.

"Instead you are here, intruding."

"TERMINATION RECOMMENDED."

"Can't you do something about that?" asked Noel.

"What is your intent?"

"My what?"

"What is your intent?"

"To return," said Noel. "Uh, to return recombined with Leon, my duplicate."

"Subject Two is not available."

Noel struggled to understand. "Subject Two . . . that's Leon?"

"The designations match."

Fresh alarm rose in Noel. "What's happened to him? Where is he?"

"Coordinates would not be comprehensible to you."

"Thanks a lot," muttered Noel, then remembered that this entity could hear every word, every thought.

"Your passage through the time stream failed."

"No kidding," said Noel bitterly.

"Subject Two was successful."

The alarm in Noel intensified. "You mean, he's back in the twenty-sixth century?"

The idea of Leon in the future, no doubt masquerading as Noel, sickened him. Leon would trick them into shutting the time portal, closing Noel off forever. He would be trapped here in nothingness for all eternity, unless the recommended termination occurred first.

"Your coordinates have no meaning," said the voice.

"Twenty-sixth century? Oh." Noel rephrased it. "My origin point. Is that where Subject Two has gone?"

"Negative."

"Oh, no," said Noel, his spirits sinking. "Not to colonial America. Not to the Revolution."

"These terms have no meaning."

"I was there, briefly," said Noel. "Just before I was sucked back into the time stream or here or wherever I am now. Leon is attached to me. Where I go in time, he goes also."

"Yes."

"Are you saying that's where he is?"

"Yes."

"Then I've got to get back there," said Noel worriedly. "God knows what he's up to already."

"You said your objective was to return to origin point. Now that has changed. You are not reliable."

"No, you don't understand!" said Noel. "I *must* return with him. If we don't come back together, the rip will widen and—"

"Understood."

"TERMINATION RECOMMENDED."

"You don't have to terminate me," said Noel hastily.

"You have intruded."

"It was unintentional. I did materialize, then something happened. I'm not sure—"

"Imprecision is a hallmark of your technology."

"Time in itself is not precise," Noel snapped.

"Error."

"Who says? There isn't a clock on the planet that doesn't slip fractionally over the course of days, months, years. We're dependent on planet rotation, and that varies. The universe fluctuates constantly, creating and decaying. You can tick along just so far and then you have to make adjustments. So don't hand me any crap about precision."

The voice remained silent.

Noel smirked to himself. It seemed he had finally won a point.

"Your journeys into time alarm us," said the voice finally. "We have stood aside without interference, but now you have interfered with us. You are a danger of great magnitude. You cannot continue."

Noel waited for the blast of termination recommended, but it didn't come. Maybe his contact had finally turned the damned thing off.

"I wish you no harm," said Noel. "We travel in order to learn. We are trying to save ourselves and our civilization from decay."

"You are disordered. You meddle with things that you barely understand. You are dangerous."

"I am trying to repair the damage," said Noel. "If you terminate me, then the damage will continue. The anomaly can only be repaired if I am recombined with Leon."

"You have substantiated this method?"

The voice was almost as bad as Dr. Rugle, wanting proof and tests for everything. Noel didn't need tests. He knew the answer inside his heart and soul. He would trust his own instincts over empirical formulas and hypotheses every time.

"Yet your instincts are merely hypotheses," said the voice.

Noel jumped. "Damn! Do you have to read my mind?"

"Communication is constant, despite its variety of forms."

Noel started to reply to that, then stopped himself.

"There is something persuasive in your appeal," said the voice as though reluctantly.

"What can I say to convince you?"

"I must think."

For an instant the darkness seemed to grow blacker. Solitude was a cold, empty hell. "Don't leave me!" Noel called out.

"You are afraid?"

Noel wrestled with himself a moment. "Yeah," he finally said. "If you go, there's nothing here."

The darkness immediately around his consciousness point faded to a misty gray. He saw a face shimmering within the currents, vaguely glimpsed like a dim reflection in a pond. It was not a human face, yet there was nothing frightening about it. Two luminous eyes, a mouth, an oval shape to the head. The ears were set high on its skull, and pointed. It lacked hair of any kind.

"I am Qwip," said the voice.

"I'm Noel." He hesitated, then ventured to add, "I thought you'd look like us."

"Human?"

"Yes."

"I am human," said Qwip.

"But you—" Noel stopped, afraid to finish his sentence.

"You do not see me," said Qwip. "You lack sufficient references. I have reached into your subconsciousness and pulled forth this image. It will suffice, since you lack comprehension. You are insufficiently advanced mentally and physically for time travel. You venture blindly into forces that you cannot control. You seek to unleash energies too strong for your abilities."

"Okay, enough of the lecture," said Noel. "You're on my side, aren't you? You believe me, don't you? Let me go back and try to get Leon. Please."

"My people are alarmed," said Qwip. "They are against this course of action."

"But you understand, don't you?" pleaded Noel. "Don't you?"

"I understand."

"Let me go back. Success is as important to me as it is to you."

"You have admitted you are the cause of the decay in the time stream. More of you will intrude. We cannot allow that."

"If I can fix the anomaly, the time stream will be okay. We won't be able to reach you."

Qwip was silent a long while. "I concur," he said finally. "You will go back."

"Yes!" said Noel excitedly.

"Constrain yourself. We cannot return you to the exact moment which you left. Do you understand?"

Noel's excitement crashed. He thought a moment. "On a different journey, to coordinates called New Mexico, I was hurt, unconscious, and I drifted from reality back into the time stream. Is that what's happening to me now?"

"Yes."

"Before, though, I returned exactly to where I was. My body was there, and it was like an astral projection—"

"No," said Qwip flatly. "You are no longer in reality. You are here."

"Between."

"Yes."

"All of me."

"Yes."

"Odd."

"Dangerous."

Noel sighed. "Can you return me?"

"Not to that coordinate."

"You mean day and hour?"

"Yes."

"But Leon is there."

"Yes."

"How long?" Noel caught himself. "Never mind. Of course that has no meaning here. How close to that coordinate can you return me?"

Qwip's vague features broke apart. They re-formed but less cohesively. The gloom was closing in once more. "I cannot return you," he said finally.

"Then how?"

"You must return yourself."

"But I don't—"

"You have this chance," said Qwip ominously. "If you fail, then I must seek your termination."

Noel believed him. Nevertheless he said, "You have the technology to time travel? You can cross into our dimension?"

"Our technology is different from yours."

"And it's incomprehensible. I know," said Noel caustically.

"I can reach you if you remain in the past," said Qwip. "Be warned."

"Yeah, but if I—"

Qwip vanished.

"Hey!" called Noel. "Come back! I have some more questions."

But Qwip did not return. The darkness closed in around Noel's consciousness point. He was alone once again, as lonely and insignificant as a speck of dust in outer space. Timeless, empty vastness surrounded him. He hated it. He feared it. He knew if he stayed in it for very long he would go insane.

How to go back?

His LOC didn't work here. How could it?

On other occasions when he'd lost his reference points, he'd been forced to re-create them in his mind. He did that now, trying to visualize the snowy battlefield where he'd been shot. He didn't want to go back to that place of violent destruction. He didn't want to go back to pain, possibly death. Yet to stay here meant his fate was certain.

He focused his thoughts and concentrated on cold, on snow, on the fields of long ago.

Back, he thought fiercely. *Go back.*

CHAPTER 5

Noel materialized with a jolt that left him gasping for breath. His skin tingled unpleasantly, almost painfully, as though his nerve endings had been scorched. When he first became a traveler, time travel had been a simple, almost effortless joy. All he had to do was walk through the old time portal in Lab 14 at the Institute, dissolve into the mist, and emerge on the other side with no side effect worse than occasional mild nausea or raging hunger. But this was getting to be too hard.

Coughing, he straightened from a crouch, wiped the perspiration from his face, and looked around to get his bearings.

It was all wrong.

The countryside itself seemed similar enough, in that it had cleared, rolling pastures that were bordered by forest, but the thick snow he expected to see smothering the ground had melted to thin patches in the sunshine. Only a few drifts lingered in the shade.

Alarmed, Noel swallowed and tried to calm down. So the sun had come out and melted some snow. That didn't mean he'd missed his mark.

But even as he tried to reassure himself, he knew better. Before, the trees had been bare. Now they swelled with buds. In the distance he could hear a constant rushing of a stream. The ground beneath his feet glistened with moisture.

In the first materialization, everything had been frozen and lifeless in the grip of winter. In the second, there had been autumn fog and drizzle. Now there was spring thaw. He'd missed the mark by months, perhaps even years.

Feeling hollow, Noel sat down on a stone and stared at his surroundings in a numbed daze. He seemed to be in a thinly cleared field. Someone had been picking up stones and building a fence with them, but no workers were in sight now. Beyond a distant fold of the hills, a narrow column of smoke spiraled against the blue sky. He could hear the rhythmic chopping of an axe cutting wood.

Rubbing his face, Noel tried to stay calm by going through his self-check. He might as well pretend that everything was normal. Maybe his previous materializations hadn't even happened. Maybe he'd dreamed getting shot. Noel touched his forehead and found no wound. Maybe he'd dreamed the march with the skeletons. Maybe that bizarre conversation with Qwip had never occurred.

Maybe.

He shivered with more than cold.

"LOC, activate," he said.

The LOC was programmed to automatically disguise itself in a shape or design that conformed to the era being visited. But this time there was no band, no bracelet, no woven braid of lovelocks encircling Noel's left wrist. Instead he found himself wearing a heavy gold signet ring on his left hand. He frowned at it.

"LOC?"

The ring shimmered with a pale blue nimbus, but it did not alter its shape into the usual clear-sided bracelet filled with flashing miniature fiber optics.

Noel's worry increased, and with it came a sense of sinking dismay. It was all happening again. He hadn't been able to return to the future, and now his LOC was malfunctioning.

"LOC!" he said angrily. "Damn you, don't do this to me. Activate!"

The ring grew warm on his finger and continued to shimmer "Acknowledged," it said faintly.

Noel's shoulders sagged. "Thank God," he said. "Why have you changed your shape so radically?"

The LOC did not reply.

"LOC!"

"Acknowledged."

"Respond to my question. Why have you changed your shape?"

"I am programmed with molecular shift capability."

"I *know* that. I asked why."

The LOC did not reply.

"Never mind," said Noel, abandoning that line of questioning. "Run a diagnostic on your programming. Are you malfunctioning?"

"Working . . . negative malfunction."

"Well, good. Tell me where and when I am."

The LOC hummed busily.

Noel waited, feeling slightly reassured by his argument with the device. LOCs were designed to be isomorphic, and each was programmed to conform to the personality of the traveler wearing it. Noel had always enjoyed minor arguments with his, deliberately phrasing some of his questions to confuse the computer's literal mindset. But right now, any odd deviations or other evidence of possible malfunction made him nervous.

"Okay, okay," he said after a few seconds. "You've had long enough. Identify this location."

"Affirmative."

Noel frowned. "That's an incorrect response."

"Affirmative."

"Stop! Run diagnostics. Check for malfunctions."

"Working . . . no malfunctions."

"That's a crock, pal."

The LOC shimmered. "I am not programmed to respond to rhetorical statements."

"No kidding. Get this straight. I want to know my location. I want the date. Or have you compressed yourself so small, your clock isn't running?"

"Specify . . . affirmative."

Noel stood up and walked around in a small circle. Inside he was tightening into knots, but he forced himself to keep his wits. "Okay," he said to himself. "Maybe I'm going too fast. It's been one weird travel this time. We hit the wrong location, then I was snapped in and out of the time stream, and now I'm here."

"Specify instructions."

"Wait," Noel said. He thought a moment, then drew in a sharp breath. "LOC, access your internal clock and directional codes. Pinpoint specific location coordinates, latitude and longitude, then translate them to map mode and relay information by town, county, territory, colony, or significant landmark. Follow with month, day, and year. Run."

"Working . . . Schuylkill River, Pennsylvania, approximately fifty-two miles northwest of Philadelphia and approximately seven miles north of Valley Forge—"

"Valley Forge!" said Noel in wonder. "Then I didn't dream it."

The LOC said nothing.

"Continue," said Noel impatiently.

"Date is March 31, 1778."

"March. So it *is* spring. When does Washington leave Valley Forge?"

"The next campaign against British troops occurred June—"

"Stop," said Noel. "That's good. We don't have to worry about getting into another battle. LOC, scan back to previous materialization. Give location and date according to specific instructions."

"Working . . . Germantown, Pennsylvania—"

"Stop," said Noel. He didn't need to hear more. His own memories of the bleak defeat seen in the men's faces haunted him as much as his foreshadowed visions of the walking skeletons. They were symbolic, he supposed, of the men who would die of starvation and cold at their winter quarters in Valley Forge. He realized that Leon must have also materialized somewhere in that time grid. And unless he'd been yanked back and forth through the time stream like Noel, he would have had the entire winter to wreak havoc on history.

"I wonder if I can believe what Qwip told me," Noel mused aloud.

"Specify instructions."

"I'm not talking to you." Noel squinted against the sunshine, which glittered off the snow with blinding brilliance. "LOC, scan the area for Leon, using your maximum sensor radius."

"Specify Leon."

"Hell!" said Noel in consternation. "Look in your own data banks. You know good and well who Leon is."

"Specify Leon."

"Specify your request for specifications."

The LOC was silent. Noel glared at it. "Why don't you resume your usual size? This miniaturization has squeezed your circuits."

The LOC flashed blue light. "Molecular shift lacks parameters."

"What does that mean?"

"Programming does not correlate with necessary instructions."

"Oh." Noel thought that over. Obviously there were damaged spots. He shoved down fresh worries. "Okay, you've got some black holes in there. Let's see if we can't reroute them. What parameters are you lacking?"

"Data banks on costume and apparel circa 1770–1780."

"Kind of a coincidence, isn't it?"

"I am not programmed to respond to rhetorical questions."

"Yeah, and you can't handle sarcasm either. Tell me this: Were you fully or even partially operational while I was in the time stream?"

"Affirmative."

Noel slapped his palm against a tree trunk. "That devil Qwip lied to me! Did he sabotage you?"

"Question is not sufficiently specific."

"Qwip! Did he sabotage you while I was in the time stream?"

The LOC flashed. "Alterations were made."

"What was removed?"

"Data banks 001, 101, 110, 010, 111—"

"Stop." Noel paced across the mud and back again, running his hands through his hair. Whatever Qwip was, and whatever he was up to, he had lied and he had meddled. Noel was beginning to have a chilling suspicion that the rip in time might have created access for Qwip's kind. And if they were hostile, they could perhaps destroy or damage Noel's own time line.

He stared across the pasture with unseeing eyes. "I've got to find Leon and close the access point. LOC, can you shift yourself back into that, uh, braid of hair that you used during our last travel?"

"Unknown."

"Try."

The signet ring on Noel's finger grew uncomfortably hot, but he dared not move, fearing to upset the LOC's attempt to reroute its damaged circuitry. When it finally burned him, he gritted his teeth for a moment, then said sharply, "LOC, stop activity!"

The LOC stopped flashing. Gripping his hand and trying not to swear, Noel plunged it into the snow to ease the burn. The icy cold shocked away some of the pain. After a few moments, he dropped the handful of melting snow and examined his hand. The flesh on his finger was puffy and red. A second-degree burn, and the LOC had not been able to shift its disguise.

Noel swore under his breath for several seconds and cradled his aching hand against his chest. "LOC," he said at last.

It flashed, more dimly than before. "Acknowledged."

"Abandon shift attempts."

"Acknowledged."

"Scan for Leon. Your memory banks can supply you with the necessary data. If not, seek a man who is my duplicate. Give this function priority. Reroute other energy levels if necessary."

The LOC didn't respond for several seconds, then it flashed faintly. "Acknowledged."

"Repeat my instructions."

The LOC did so. Noel nodded, satisfied for the moment.

"If we're lucky, he'll show up. He usually does, but we've never encountered interference like this before. I can't trust to chance."

"I am not programmed to respond to rhetorical statements."

"Just find Leon and do it fast," said Noel.

"Acknowledged."

The sound of hoofbeats sent Noel scurrying for cover. "Deactivate," he whispered.

Too much undergrowth had been cleared from beneath the trees for them to offer a hiding place. Noel glimpsed a horse and rider being pursued by two others, both wearing scarlet.

"Hell," said Noel and flung himself behind the half-constructed stone fence.

The quarry was a civilian in breeches and top boots, wrapped in a stout woolen cloak, his head covered with a tall tricorne hat. Old or young, Noel could not tell. But the man's fear and desperation were made plain by the way he kept whipping his lathered horse and glancing over his shoulder. His mount was clearly exhausted, for it stumbled frequently. Its nostrils flared scarlet, snorting forth its breath in white plumes.

One of the soldiers fired a pistol. "Halt!" he shouted. "In the name of the king, I order you to stop!"

The shot went wide, echoing across the hills. The civilian made no effort to obey. Instead, he crouched lower over the saddle and whipped his horse hard. He wrenched his mount off the road and came thundering across the field toward Noel's hiding place.

Furious with alarm, Noel crouched lower, unable to believe his bad luck. Why did they have to come this way? The ground was shaking from the galloping hooves. Mud flew into the air. The horse was making a groaning noise deep in its lungs, and the man astride it was sobbing in his fear.

Despite his wish to avoid involvement, which in this case could end up getting him shot just because he was there, Noel's sympathy couldn't help but be touched by the man's plight. Whatever he'd done or for whatever reason the soldiers were chasing him, two against one was hardly fair. Besides that, some surprising chord of patriotism suddenly gripped Noel. It was astonishing because had he even thought about it, he would have expected the span of centuries to be too great between his time and this, but there must be something genetic, some inherited national memory of the Revolution that had stuck despite the march of time. Or else he was just thinking about that first materialization in this century when the British soldier had shot him in the head.

Either way, recklessness rose in Noel. He glanced around and picked up a pair of fist-sized stones, one for each hand.

The horse was still coming straight at the fence. *Stupid*, thought Noel. *The old guy was going to get cornered here.*

But the horse didn't slow, for he was still being whipped, kicked, and urged on by the desperate cries of his rider.

Noel realized they were going to jump, and right over where he was hiding. He tried to scuttle out of the way, but it was too late.

The horse gathered itself with a final effort and sailed over both fence and Noel. He had a confused instant of its overwhelming size, the stench of horse sweat, the scarlet flare of the beast's nostrils, and the white gleam of its eye. Lethal hooves were tucked up against the animal's undercarriage, ready to strike. There was mud clinging to the soles of the rider's boots. Noel could have reached up and touched the saddle girth.

Then they were over, and Noel could draw breath again. But the horse stumbled and fell, going down in a violent tumble of animal and rider. There was no time to react; the redcoats were at the fence.

"Ho!" yelled one, laughing. He swung his crop, and his horse rose at the fence.

Shrieking like a madman, Noel bolted upright in front of the horse and waved his arms. The animal shied and tossed its rider. The other plunged to one side, snorting with fear. Shouting in surprise, the still-mounted soldier tried to regain control of his mount. Noel threw one of his rocks. His aim was true; it hit the man in the temple, knocking off his hat. A burst of crimson splashed across his face. He toppled from his saddle.

A pistol ball whizzed a scant inch over Noel's head. He whirled, his heart thudding, and faced the other soldier.

The man was on his knees, covered with mud, and holding the smoking pistol. "You—"

Noel hurled his remaining rock and hit the soldier in the chest. He fell back with a surprised look on his face and writhed about, wheezing for air. Noel rushed to him and knocked him out.

Then all was suddenly, shockingly quiet. Breathing hard more from adrenaline rush than from actual exertion, Noel wiped the sweat from his face and stepped back. The scene had gone from a newly cleared pasture to a miniature battlefield in a matter of minutes. The two British horses trotted around with their reins dangling, too well trained to run away entirely, but still snorting and rolling their eyes in alarm. The civilian horse lay where it had fallen. Whether it had broken a leg or burst its heart, Noel couldn't say. It looked dead to him, and the civilian lay unmoving beside it.

Noel took the pistols from the redcoats. Both weapons were still slightly warm to the touch and the reek of gunpowder smoked lightly in their muzzles. One was finely made of walnut and chased silver. Although he had no ammunition for either, Noel stuck the pistols in his pockets and felt better. His little David and Goliath act had succeeded, thanks to the natural skittishness of horses and the element of surprise, but he'd rather have a gun in his hand than a rock any day.

Approaching the civilian warily, Noel stared at him for a moment. He was lying facedown and didn't stir even when Noel prodded him gently with his foot. His hat had fallen partially across his face, twisting his wig awry, and both his hands were in sight. Noel crouched beside him and put a hand on his shoulder.

"Hey," he said. "Are you able to hear me? Wake up."

He shook the man, who groaned and made a feeble movement with one hand before falling still again.

Concerned, Noel rolled the civilian onto his back and pulled the tricorne and wig away. The man's face was ashen against the trampled snow and mud, and a trickle of blood ran from the corner of his mouth.

Noel felt for broken bones and found a spongy place in the man's side. When he pressed there, the man groaned and opened his eyes. They were wild with fear and pain.

"Easy," said Noel. "You're hurt inside. Don't try to move."

The man started coughing blood, and Noel hastily sat him up so he could breathe. Close up, he looked to be in his middle forties, going soft along the jaw and in the paunch. His clothes were of good quality, although not flashy.

"Tyrants," he muttered. "Oppressors—"

"Don't try to talk," said Noel. "You need all the breath you can get."

The man's eyes fluttered closed, then opened again. They were blue and clouded with shock. "Not British—"

"Nope, I'm your fairy godfather," said Noel with a flippancy that didn't cover the worry growing inside him. What was he going to do with this man? For all he knew the fellow was supposed to be shot and hanged by the British, but here he was tampering with history again. And how was he going to get the man medical assistance? With these questions running through his mind, he pressed a reassuring hand to the man's shoulder. "Don't worry. I'm a patriot too. I'm on your side."

"God be praised," whispered the man in simple relief. He slumped.

"Oh, no you don't," said Noel. "Come on. Keep awake. Do you live near here? Do you have neighbors?"

The man's eyes rolled back in his head and his expression went slack, but Noel gave him a shake that brought him back to consciousness. "Talk to me," said Noel sharply. "Do you live around here? Where can I get help for you?"

"Sally," the man whispered, then began coughing again. "Must tell her the—must tell—"

"Sally," said Noel. "Where's Sally?"

The man's eyes were losing focus. He flung out one hand and lapsed into unconsciousness. Frustrated, Noel felt his pulse and found it racing. His skin felt clammy and cold, too cold even for having lain on the ground. But it seemed he had tried to point the direction. Noel squinted that way. No houses were in sight, but he remembered he had seen smoke earlier. Someone had to live fairly close by.

Easing the man to the ground, he scrubbed the blood off his hands and set himself to catch one of the British horses. One shied off completely, but the other one let him approach. He stroked its neck, making soothing noises, and the animal tossed its head. As soon as he grasped the dangling reins, the animal nuzzled him affectionately and snorted all over his shoes.

Tying the horse to a tree, Noel kept a wary eye on the two unconscious soldiers and unsaddled the horse quickly. It took some effort to pull the civilian's saddle off the dead horse, but he finally managed to drag it free. Putting it on the British horse, he then struggled to heave the civilian across it. There came no sound, although he was rougher in handling the fellow than he meant to be. Noel patted his back in apology.

Unlacing the civilian's saddlebags, Noel dug through a few personal effects, finding an extra pair of gloves that he drew on gladly, a purse of money, which he appropriated, and a hunk of bread and cheese swathed in a clean cloth. Munching on this, Noel almost overlooked a thin packet wrapped in oilskin. Inside there was a letter written in florid copperplate on heavy parchment paper. It was a note of safe conduct, and it was signed by Benjamin Franklin of the Continental Congress. The second sheet contained a list of dates and names that meant nothing to Noel, but he suspected this was dangerous information for anyone to be carrying across a country at war.

No wonder his civilian had been pursued by soldiers.

Don't get into this, warned a small voice in Noel's head. *You have your own agenda.*

Sighing, Noel wrapped up the papers once again in the oilskin and made a swift cut in the saddle pad. He crammed the packet inside and pulled some of the stuffing to the edge of the cut to conceal what lay inside it. Then he led the horse and its unconscious burden toward help.

The house over the hill was no mansion, but it was finer than an ordinary farmstead. Built of gray stone with a sloped slate roof and large windows, it stood partway up a rise of ground, with a small pond in front of it and a snug set of barns and outbuildings to the rear. There was a walled garden at the side, and Noel came walking through an orchard on his way to the house.

Geese were the first to sound the alarm at his approach. Hissing and honking, they waddled forward, only to be scattered by a pack of barking dogs. Having no desire to get his leg bitten, Noel stopped where he was and tightened his grip on the nervous horse's bridle.

"Hello!" he shouted.

A shout echoed back to him. In a moment a boy of about fourteen, clad in a leather jerkin and linen shirt, came out from behind the house with an axe in his hands. He stopped beside the picket fence enclosing the front garden.

"Is Sally about?" asked Noel, taking a gamble.

The boy's stance relaxed. "Oh, aye," he said and cupped his hand to his mouth. "Ho! Sally, come out!"

"Call off your dogs," said Noel.

"Bouncer! Lad! Tulip! Come away," said the boy.

At once the dogs scattered and trotted off, losing interest in Noel at once. The geese, however, were not so easily mollified. Noel kicked his way through them, aware that the boy was amused by how the gander stretched his neck and spread his wings aggressively. The birds' hissing did not amuse Noel, who expected to have a plug nipped from his hide at any moment.

By the time he reached the front of the house, a young woman with her blond hair swept up becomingly and a shawl tied about her shoulders had appeared on the front steps. She hastened forward at the sight of him.

"What's happened?" she cried. "You left us not an hour ago, and here you are come again. And in such clothes as these. Is it a spy you've become, Lieutenant Nardek?"

At the name, Noel's blood congealed in his veins. He stood there a moment, then took a half step forward. "You know—"

"And who's this you've brought in all bloody?" she asked, unheeding.

The boy, equally blond and blue-eyed, was obviously her younger brother. He lifted the unconscious man's head and gasped. "Lord, Sally! It's Peterson."

"Peterson!" she echoed. The color left her cheeks and she cast Noel an odd, frightened glance before glaring at the boy. "Hush, Robert, of course it's not. You're mistaken. We don't know this man at all."

"Are you sure?" asked Noel. "He told me to seek out a Sally. That's your name, isn't it?"

She flinched, her eyes staring at him with a look that was agonizing to see. "In God's name, don't toy with us like this."

"Do you know him or not?" persisted Noel. He glanced at the boy, who was looking nearly as frightened as the girl. "Look, forget your politics for a moment. The man's badly hurt. He may die."

She drew an unsteady breath and gripped her hands together against her stomach. "What happened to him?"

"His horse threw him," said Noel, deciding not to mention the soldiers just yet. "I happened to be on the spot and thought he'd better have help. Is there a doctor in these parts?"

"Aye," said the boy, looking puzzled. "But seeing as you played whist with Dr. Selincourt last night here in our own parlor, I wonder why you ask such a question."

"Never mind," said Sally, throwing Noel yet another worried look. "Let's get him into the house as quick as we can. Have Silas help you, Robert. Lieutenant, will you—"

"You'd better send the boy for the doctor as fast as he can ride," said Noel. "I'll help get Peterson inside."

"Very well. Take the chestnut when you go, Robert. He's the fastest. And mind you bundle up well. The wind is still sharp."

Still looking frightened, she gave Noel a perfunctory smile and hastened into the house. He heard her calling for servants. By the time he managed to drag Peterson off the horse, a large black man in homespun appeared to help carry the injured man inside. Between them they got him upstairs and into a cold bedchamber with a sloped ceiling.

"I'll get a fire started," said Silas.

By then Sally appeared with a strip of bandages in her hands. "The water's heating," she said without preamble.

Noel wanted to explain to her that he was not his twin, with whom she was obviously already well acquainted. But it didn't seem to be the right moment for awkward explanations.

"I'll see to the horse," he said.

She nodded, but he noticed how she avoided looking directly at him. Her hands, as she unfastened Peterson's coat, were shaking.

He returned outside and led the horse into the barn. Finding a stall, he stripped off saddle and bridle and gave the horse some water. Slinging the saddlebags over his shoulder, he walked back inside the house.

It was a rambling, comfortable place. He glimpsed a rather grand parlor filled with formal wingback chairs and mahogany tables. Past the imposing curve of the staircase lay a hall leading to the rear of the house. Exiting, he stepped along a path of flagstones to a humble log structure. It was there that the woodsmoke was rising from a brick chimney. Delicious smells of baking bread made his mouth water.

Following his nose, and his growling stomach, Noel entered the kitchen.

A thin woman with red hair twisted on top of her head was bustling between open fire, brick oven, and a huge table filled with preparations. A child of about three clung to her skirts, and a younger one waved a wooden rattle from where he'd been tied in a chair with a dishcloth.

"Hello," said Noel quietly, not wanting to startle her. "Any chance of a bite?"

She whirled just the same, and her face grew pinched at the sight of him. "You, is it?" she said with open insolence. "Well, you came back speedily enough, and in a new suit of clothes too. Did you decide to sell out your colors, Lieutenant, or are you playing spy today?"

The idea that Leon had been here earlier was frustrating. Noel didn't answer her question. Instead he looked around with longing. "That coffee smells good."

"And if you expect to get any, you may think again. I've too much to do to be wasting my time with the likes of you. Miss Sally may tolerate you for the major's sake, but you're no better than you should be. Now clear out of my kitchen before the pastries are burned."

"Hannah!" said a soft voice, sounding shocked. "How roughly you speak to our guest, to be sure."

Noel turned and found himself face-to-face with Sally. Up close, she was lovely indeed, with the kind of bone structure that would retain beauty all her life. A clear milk-and-roses complexion, intelligent blue eyes, slim arched brows, and hair like spun gold were enough to make his senses spin. She also possessed a figure curved and full in all the right places, slim everywhere else. Her dress was fashioned of a soft, plain blue wool with a cut and sophistication that said it must have been ordered from London. She wore a filmy white fichu crossed over her bosom, and her shawl hung from her elbows.

He realized he was staring, flushed, and scrambled to find his manners. "I'm sorry," he said. "I didn't mean to—"

But she was staring back with an arrested expression in her eyes. A tiny frown appeared between her brows. She raised one slender hand to silence him and said, "You aren't Lieutenant Nardek, after all. I thought you were at first, in all the excitement. But you aren't."

The cook put her hands on her hips and looked at first one of them and then the other. "Miss Sally! What kind of maggot do you have in your head now? Not the lieutenant? Why, when anyone can plainly see—"

"No," said Sally. Her clear gaze never wavered from Noel's. And there was anger in her frown, anger and bewilderment instead of the relief he expected. "Not Nardek."

No lie in the world, no matter how skilled, was going to convince her otherwise. And Noel didn't intend to lie.

"No," he said quietly. "I'm not Leon Nardek."

CHAPTER 6

Widening her eyes, Sally said nothing.

Hannah screamed and dropped the pitcher she was holding. White milk splashed upon the earthen floor, and both babies began to cry.

"Oh, make them hush, Hannah, do," said Sally crossly. Her blue eyes flashed to Noel. "You'd better step outside with me and explain yourself, sir."

"Miss Sally, don't you dare go anywhere with that man!" said Hannah fiercely. She snatched up a broom and brandished it at Noel. "I knew you were up to no good. I—"

"Hush," said Sally with a sharpness in her tone that caught Hannah up short. She looked at Noel again and walked outside.

He followed, with a final longing look at the pastries cooling from the oven. The bread and cheese he'd eaten earlier had been stale, and had only staved off the intense hunger brought on by traveling, not satisfied it.

The young woman ahead of him walked with an angry stride that sent her skirts flying about her ankles. She walked to the far end of the garden, out of earshot of both the house and the kitchen, and turned to face him beneath the swelling branches of a pear tree.

"Now, sir. I am Sally Crewe, mistress of this house and land," she said curtly. "I want your name and an honest explanation of how Peterson came to be so grievously injured and in your care."

"My name is Noel Kedran. I—"

"And your relation to Lieutenant Nardek?" she demanded. "You're as like to him as a twin."

"You're pretty observant to be able to tell us apart," said Noel. "I've come here looking for him. I hope you'll be able to tell me where—"

"That will do for later, when I know you're not a scoundrel. Thus far all I know is that you've come on my property under false pretenses."

She was as prickly as she was pretty, and her high tone aroused Noel's own irritation. He said, "Peterson is probably going to die. In trying to get him some medical attention, I didn't see any need to stand around and tell everyone who I really was. I've been mistaken for Leon before."

"Yes, and used it for your advantage, I'll wager."

Noel's face heated in spite of himself. "The reverse would be truer, Miss Crewe."

"How so? The lieutenant is Major Burton's adjutant and an able officer. He is received everywhere and well liked. You look like a vagrant."

As she spoke, she swept him with a contemptuous gaze. Noel glanced down at himself and realized that with his breeches muddy, his stockings torn, and his coat ripped, he couldn't look very trustworthy.

"I've come a long way to find Leon," was all he said.

"And your business with Peterson?"

He frowned. "I was minding my own business when he came along. He was being chased by a pair of soldiers."

"Soldiers!" she said in alarm. "But—"

"I sort of, um, stepped in," said Noel. "But his horse fell with him. He landed pretty hard. I figure he's broken several ribs and has internal injuries. He needs—"

"Are you a doctor?" she broke in.

"No."

"Then let us not discuss what you think he needs."

"Listen—"

"No, you listen to me. What happened to those soldiers? What did you do?"

Noel sent her a sideways look and didn't answer.

She began to pace back and forth, wringing her hands. "There'll be trouble for this . . . retaliations. They'll come searching. You've put us all in danger."

Noel gritted his teeth, furious with her cool, callous disregard of anything but herself. "And I should have let him die in the mud?" he said angrily. "Your friend?"

She gasped. "He is *not*—"

"Really," said Noel with scorn. "Not your friend, though he said your name with his last conscious breath—"

"Stop!" she cried and pressed her hands to her scarlet cheeks. Turning away, she stood for a moment in an effort to compose herself, then glanced over her shoulder. "You make me sound like a monster."

Noel said nothing. His silence brought her around.

Her face went white with fury. "I don't know who you are or by what reason you have come here, and I don't wish to know. You're a scoundrel, probably a deserter from Washington's army. You do not belong here, and you will not be given shelter or money or whatever it is you hope to gain. You will leave my property now, or I'll have Silas throw you off. Is that clear?"

Noel glared at her. "I told you I'm looking for Leon Nardek. If you'll tell me where to find him, I'll go."

She looked right through him and held out her hand. "Why don't you give me Peterson's saddlebags first."

He'd forgotten he was still carrying them. From her tone it was plain she thought him a thief on top of everything else.

Shrugging them off, he handed them to her, then did a slow burn while she opened them and checked the contents.

"I ate his lunch," said Noel through his teeth. "I'm hungry. My last meal was a turnip."

He saw her hand pause inside the saddlebag. Her whole body tensed, but when she looked up at him her expression was as cool as ever. "No doubt you're planning a hearty meal indeed at the tavern when you come to it," she said in a very angry voice. "You've taken all his money, haven't you?"

Her face was still pale, making her eyes stand out bluer than ever. In spite of her anger there was a tremble in her hands and a quaver in her voice. This girl had plenty of courage and spirit, but she was badly frightened.

Noel refused to make it easy on her. "Aren't you more concerned about some papers he was carrying?"

She drew in her breath sharply, then something gave in her face and she swayed.

He caught her, but she rallied almost at once, striking his shoulder with her fist and trying to twist free of his supporting arm. "Unhand me, you blackguard!" she cried. "How dare you—"

"Shut up," said Noel.

He manhandled her over to a wooden bench beneath an arbor now devoid of any roses and pushed her onto it.

"You—"

"I said shut up."

She snapped her mouth shut and glared at him a moment, then pressed her hands to her face.

"I've got the paper," he said without mercy, although a part of him hated to break her spirit.

She pushed her hands down to her lap and clenched them. She was still shaking. "What do you mean to do with it?" she asked.

"I don't know yet."

That seemed to surprise her more than anything. "I don't understand you, sir, but please don't play games with me."

"I'm not playing a game," he said grimly. "All I want is to find my twin. I concealed the paper because it looked dangerous."

She shot him a swift, speculative glance before lowering her lashes. "Then you read it?"

"Maybe."

"Why," she asked with great care, her earlier haughtiness gone, "are you seeking the lieutenant? Will you betray Peterson?"

"He's a friend of yours, isn't he?"

"Peterson," she said, swallowing hard, "is my uncle's courier."

"And your uncle?"

"Why, he's John Crewe, of Philadelphia. Everyone in Pennsylvania knows him."

"I'm not from Pennsylvania."

She lowered her gaze again. "He's a member of the Continental Congress."

"You say that as though you're ashamed of it."

Her eyes flashed, but she said nothing, even when he frowned at her. The haughty look that he didn't like returned to her face. Her eyes grew defiant.

"I see," he said finally.

"You have no business to criticize my sentiments in this stupid war," she said angrily.

"No."

"There are few enough here who sympathize with traitors to the king."

"Really? Even with General Washington's troops so close?"

Her cheeks grew pink. "Those incompetents. Most of them have starved."

"Is that their fault?" he asked. "Or can we blame congressmen like your uncle who won't give Washington the supplies or the support he needs?"

"You can go!"

"Not until you tell me where to find Leon."

"Why should I tell you anything? Why should I help you?"

"You'd like to have the paper, wouldn't you?"

Her chin lowered. The anger in her eyes came back under control. She looked at him with so much speculation he laughed.

"No schemes necessary, Miss Crewe. An even exchange. The paper in return for the information."

She frowned at him. "And that is all you want?"

"Yes."

"All?"

"What else do you think I should ask for?"

She jumped to her feet and glared at him. "Oh, you are impertinent, sir! If you think—"

"I don't think anything," he broke in, tired of her dramatics. "I'm trying to find my brother."

"Is he your brother?" she asked. "You don't have the same name."

"Brothers don't always."

Her eyebrows swept up. "Then who was born on the wrong side of the blanket, him or you? Considering the color in your face, sir, I think I have my answer."

"You're wrong," he snapped, goaded in spite of himself.

"Am I? Why, then, does Lieutenant Nardek have a commission in His Majesty's army? Why is he an officer and a gentleman? Why is he received everywhere in society? Why is he favored among his fellow officers and friends? Why all this? As for you—"

"Little girls shouldn't judge by appearances," muttered Noel.

The look she shot him was all scorn. "Appearances speak plainly enough. You will find your brother billeted in town, at the home of Mr. Ezekiel Smyth. Now that paper, if you please."

"Come with me," said Noel.

In silence they walked to the barn. He pulled the thin packet from its hiding place in the saddle pad and handed it to her.

She took it as though amazed that it could be that easy. "Did you find it in this place? You are a clever searcher."

"I found it in his saddlebags, along with his lunch," said Noel. "How far to town, and in which direction?"

"I have given you all the information I agreed to."

He glared at her a moment and met nothing but saucy defiance in her eyes. Without another word he walked out and started down the lane past the gauntlet of barking dogs and hissing geese.

He was nearly to the road before she shouted and came running after him like a little girl, with her skirts flashing up nearly to her knees. He stopped and she caught up with him in a whirl of shawl and petticoats, breathless and prettier than ever.

"You are an odd man indeed, sir," she said, panting. "I'm sorry I did not thank you for helping Peterson. If he lives, it will be due to your kindness."

This sudden expression of gratitude surprised him. Before he meant to, he smiled at her. "Glad to do it."

She smiled back and pointed. "Town lies that way. It's two miles, no farther."

"Thank you." He hesitated. "And there will be trouble for you. I wasn't thinking of that at the time."

She lifted her chin proudly. "We shall manage."

He looked at her but there was nothing else to say. With a nod, he walked on.

"Go first to the Yellow Duck," she called after him. "It's a brick tavern, new and at the crossroads. The lieutenant is often there, and if not his friends will direct you."

Noel waved and started down the road.

He had to walk briskly to keep himself nominally warm. Although the sun was bright, the wind was very cold and his breath hung in a mist about his face. He met a carriage, then a cart, then a few people on horseback. A squadron of British soldiers galloped past him, forcing him off the road altogether. Splashed with their mud, Noel waited until they were far ahead of him before returning to the road. At least they hadn't questioned him, and he was glad of that because he didn't have a story prepared yet.

The American Revolution had supposedly been Dr. Rugle's specialty before she gave up history for administration. He'd always had a casual idea that Americans were banded together against the hated British, but in this prosperous little town everyone seemed on good terms. These people must be Tory sympathizers, for the most part, imagining themselves loyal subjects to their king and possibly still considering themselves to be English. Odd indeed, when he knew Washington's men were starving and suffering only a few miles away for a cause that would give these people more freedom than they could handle.

When he entered town, he checked at the tavern Sally had mentioned, but Leon was not there. The innkeeper gave him a peculiar look, and Noel left quickly.

He went into a bun shop and bought himself lunch. When he was full and thawed, he explored the town. The houses were mostly brick or stone, well-built Georgian or Dutch structures with shutters and slate roofs. Merchants stood about, looking prosperous as they chatted with customers. The ringing bells of shop doors could be heard up and down the central street. Traffic moved at a placid pace. Children were indoors, presumably at their lessons. Boy apprentices hurried past on errands. British soldiers lounged here and there, idly playing dice or reading letters to each other or flirting with the young ladies who were walking with their chaperones. Other than the bright uniforms, war seemed to have passed this community by.

Deciding he needed new clothes, Noel stepped into a tailor's shop. It was warm from a fire busily crackling on the hearth. The windows and wainscoting were painted a merry blue. Neat bolts of cloth were stacked on shelves. And a ready-made brown coat hung in the shop window. Noel looked at it, trying to decide if it would fit.

"Hello, sir," said the tailor, emerging from the back with a brisk step. He faltered when he saw Noel.

"Hi," said Noel. "I guess it's obvious what I'm here for. My clothes have had it. Got anything that will fit me?"

The tailor went on staring at him in open consternation.

Noel was getting tired of this kind of reaction. "I have money to pay you," he said sharply. "Can you fit me?"

"I—I daresay," said the tailor. He made no effort to come any closer.

Soldiers marched past outside, their footsteps in cadence. The tailor stared at them through the window and wrung his hands.

"You should not be here," he said at last, almost in a moan. "You'll be arrested if you're noticed."

Noel rolled his eyes. "Look, I'm muddy and I'm cold. I'd like some decent clothes. I can pay for them. Are you going to wait on me, or not?"

The tailor stared at him with terrified eyes. "You may be willing to take the risk, but I'm not. You'd better go."

"I'm not who you think I am—"

"Aren't you?" said the man. "Good heavens, man, it's obvious you're a deserter. Look at you, ragged and desperate. But if they catch you, you'll be shot as a spy at the very least."

"I'm not a spy."

"Where's your uniform, then?"

"And if I had one on," said Noel in exasperation, "wouldn't that advertise—"

"Yes, indeed. I hadn't thought of that. Only go, I pray you! I daren't be caught abetting a traitor."

Noel glared at him. "Is it against the law to sell me a coat?"

The tailor stared at him like a rabbit.

"Well?"

The tailor jumped. "Indeed, I don't know. I don't want the trouble. I dare not take the risk. I have a family, young children to feed. My wife is expecting another—"

"Forget it," said Noel. He opened the door to leave and backed up as a burly soldier in a powdered wig and red uniform walked inside, brushing past him rudely.

"Marley, have you finished my order yet?" demanded the soldier. "I have been waiting all week. You know the ball is tomorrow night."

"Lieutenant Fox," stammered the tailor, backing up behind his counter. "Indeed, sir, I haven't forgotten. It's almost finished."

"Almost! Gad, you have the slowest fingers on this earth. London tailors would have had my coat ready in a twinkling, half the time it takes you to sew on a dashed button."

"I'm sorry. I told you it would take time to procure the buttons from Philadelphia. Such particular details—"

"Make the coat, Marley. Make the coat. Gad, you colonials and your provincial ideas."

Yawning, the soldier leaned on the counter and let his eyes rove around the shop to where Noel still stood by the window. "And who are you?"

Marley started nervously. "Just a vagrant, sir. Nothing to signify. I've told him to leave. He was just going when you came in."

"Begging is against the law," said the soldier, looking Noel up and down with a frowning eye.

"I wasn't begging," said Noel.

"Impertinent too!" said the lieutenant. He straightened up and gripped Noel by the arm. His fingers were like iron. "Out you go, you rascal."

Yanking open the door, he shoved Noel down the steps to the street. At the side of the shop between the buildings, he pushed Noel against the wall.

Not sure whether he was going to have to fight or run for it, Noel turned about and found the soldier grinning at him.

"Leon, you sly devil," he said with delight. "I don't know what rig Burton's got you up to, and I don't want to know. None of my affair if you've turned spy. Damned good outfit. You look like one of Washington's scarecrows, only a little too fat."

"I—"

Still chuckling, the lieutenant clapped him on the shoulder and strolled back into the shop.

When the door slammed shut, Noel leaned his head against the wall and shut his eyes for a moment. Leon had certainly made himself known. It was disconcerting to keep running into his friends.

Squeezing himself deeper into the alley, Noel crouched behind a set of side steps where he could remain unseen. Stripping off his gloves, he brought his signet ring close to his lips.

"LOC, activate," he whispered.

The ring grew warm on his burned finger.

Noel winced. "Any sign of Leon?"

"Negative."

"I wish the fool still had his LOC. He'd be easy to trace." Only God knew what kind of havoc Leon would have caused with it.

"Please specify instructions."

"Have you found any evidence of tampering with history?"

"I have received no such instructions. Please specify."

Noel sighed. "This is not my day. Look, we don't have time to mess around. Usually you're yelling about anomalies and altered history or giving me warnings. What about it?"

"I will scan," said the LOC austerely.

It hummed busily for a while.

"Well?" demanded Noel finally.

"Parameters are too vague."

Noel groaned and rested his forehead on his knees.

"Are you ill, sir?" asked a kindly voice.

Startled, Noel jumped to his feet and whirled around.

He found himself face to face with Sally Crewe's little brother. The boy was lean and gawky, lacking his sister's grace. He was as fair as she, his features honest and goodwilled. He seemed as astonished to see Noel as Noel was to see him.

"Mr. Nardek," he said and smiled. "I found the doctor and sent him on to the farm. I thought you'd still be out there."

Noel hid his left hand at his side and hoped the LOC wouldn't volunteer any information on its own. "No, I had to come in. I—I don't know your name, boy."

The boy frowned. "Don't know my—I beg your pardon. Are you hoaxing me? Of course you know me. Good heavens, you saw me not an hour ago. I'm Robert Crewe."

Noel could have kicked himself for forgetting the boy's name and giving himself away. Still, it seemed he was doomed to constantly repeat his explanation.

"You're wrong," he said impatiently. "I'm not Leon. I'm his brother."

"Jupiter!" said Robert in awe. "Are you, sir? You look ever so like him. When you came up to the house, big as life, I naturally thought—"

"There was too much confusion for introductions. My name is Kedran."

"Oh, I'm sorry I mistook you, Mr. Kedran." The boy put out his hand to shake. "But you're very like him."

"Twins."

"Yes, I can see that now. How odd. But you aren't an officer, are you, sir?"

"No. Not on the British side either."

Robert glanced around. "Please, sir, not so loud. It pays to be careful around these Tories."

"Your sister's one."

Robert turned red and looked at his feet. "I know. I've tried my best to reason with her, but she won't listen. You won't give away her game, will you, sir?"

Noel didn't have any idea of what he was talking about, but there wasn't any point in saying so. He slipped his left hand into his pocket. "No, I won't give her away."

"Thank you! Only, why are you in the alley if you're looking for Lieutenant Nardek?"

Noel slung his arm around the boy's shoulders. "That is a very good question. Why don't I ask you one first?"

Robert's blue eyes were guileless and steady. "Of course."

"Do you like my brother?"

Robert's face flamed red again.

"No, please be honest. I won't be offended either way."

"But he's Major Burton's adjutant. I can't say."

"You already have," said Noel gently. He took his arm from the boy's shoulders.

Robert looked agitated. "You've tricked an answer from me, but I've said nothing against him. I—"

"Hey, it's okay," said Noel. "I don't like him much either."

"Then why are you looking for him?"

"It's a family matter. My, uh, father wants him to come home."

"Jupiter!" said Robert, looking much impressed. "All the way to England?"

"Yes, it's a very long way home."

"But if he's needed, sir, why don't you just go to his commanding officer and relay the message that your brother must sell out? I'm sure Major Burton would understand. He's pretty decent, after all."

"I thought you weren't a Tory."

Robert widened his eyes. "I'm not! But I'm no traitor either."

"Ah, neutral ground, is it?"

"I have to be," said Robert, "what with Sally's—but I mustn't speak of that. I promised."

Sally, thought Noel grimly, was in intrigue up to her pretty eyebrows. He pretended not to notice what Robert's naive remarks were giving away. "Well, you have a sensible head on your shoulders, Robert. I would go to Major Burton, but I'm not dressed for calling on an officer, am I?"

Robert looked him over critically. "Well, you are a bit ragged round the edges, sir."

"Yeah, you're a born diplomat. I tried to buy myself a new suit, but the tailor didn't want my business."

Robert snorted. "Marley? He's an old ninny hammer if ever I saw one. His competition would deal with you, I'm sure."

Noel had already decided that he should stay off the streets for a while. If too many of Leon's friends saw him, word would get back to Leon quickly enough. He didn't want his twin warned.

"I have another idea," he said. "I'm going to wait for my brother in his rooms. Your sister said he lodges with Ezekiel Smyth. Can you give me directions?"

"I can do better than that. I'll show you the house."

"Thanks." Noel glanced at the busy street and headed deeper into the alley. "Let's take the back way."

Robert shot him a suspicious look. "You're kind of a rum one, aren't you, sir?"

Noel lengthened his stride so that Robert had to hurry to keep pace with him. "What did the doctor say when you sent him to Peterson?"

Robert stuck his hands in his breeches pockets and scowled.

Noel glanced at him in surprise. "Didn't you find him?"

Still Robert said nothing.

"What's the matter?"

Robert scowled more fiercely. "It's better we not talk of that, sir."

"Why not?"

"The doctor's no friend."

"What's that to do with whether he can save a man's life?"

Robert shook his head. "Who's to say what Peterson may utter in his delirium? I've warned Sally over and over not to get involved, but you know how older sisters are. She thinks I'm too little to know anything and I'm *not*."

"I never had a sister," said Noel. "Lucky, I guess."

"Oh, I don't mean to speak against Sally. She can be a great gun, but since she went into politics, well, I don't mind saying it's got me in a fret."

He looked up at Noel and his blue eyes held baffled fury. "I heard the doctor talking to Ollenby. I didn't mean to eavesdrop, but the window was open just a crack. They were—were talking about the *plot* and—"

"What plot?"

Robert gripped his coat and glanced around. "Please keep your voice down, sir."

"What plot?" asked Noel more softly.

"I don't know," said Robert, but it was plain he was lying. He shot Noel an anguished look. "If they hadn't mentioned Sally's name, I wouldn't have lingered, but I *had* to listen then."

"Of course you did. What did they say?"

"I daresay I shouldn't trust you. I don't know you at all."

"Better not tell me any secrets," said Noel lightly, but he was conscious of a stab of concern. Robert was too young to be involved with the plots of war. For that matter, so was his very pretty sister. *Don't get involved*, Noel reminded himself.

"But you brought Peterson in for help. That must mean you have a kind heart. And your eyes are honest, not like your brother's at all," confided Robert naively. "It's just that they suspect Sally. I've tried to tell her she is sailing too close to the wind, but she won't listen. The major is just trifling with her affections. And she believes everything he tells her."

"Okay, so she's in love with Major Burton," said Noel, watching the street ahead of them. He crossed over and went down another alley to avoid a trio of soldiers. "What's that got to do with Peterson and the doctor you don't trust?"

Robert hunched his shoulders and looked ashamed. "I wasn't going to go in. It made me so angry I could wish Peterson at the devil. Though Lord knows, if he dies, he may end up there."

"Don't get off the subject," said Noel. "What did you tell the doctor?"

"He saw me at the window and looked no end put out. I told him as little as possible but, Jupiter, someone will put it together. Peterson is such a booby for getting hurt. He was to do no more than convey a message to Sally when he passed through the country, but now here he is laid up at the house and like to die. There'll be questions, no matter what. The major is bound to have suspicions when he hears about this, and the doctor will repeat anything Peterson blurts out."

Trouble, Sally had said. Retaliations. Noel considered it. "I seem to have done you no favor by bringing the man to your house."

"Well, it's not your fault, sir," said Robert with ready generosity. "You know nothing of this business. I just wish I hadn't come to town. I could have told Sally Dr. Selincourt wasn't to be found, and she'd have believed that. Peterson looked ready to stick his spoon in the wall, and you said it yourself that he hasn't much of a chance. Bert Myers took a toss last year and he died of it straightaway, even with the doctor there."

Noel frowned at him. "That's no reason not to try, Robert."

"I know it!" said Robert. He bit his lip. "But Peterson's a patriot, up to his neck in treason, and if they find out Sally's harboring such a fellow in the house, she'll be done for. And the major won't save her. She thinks he'd go bail for her, but I don't. It's just too big of a risk, sir. Don't you see?"

Noel saw very well. Revolt wasn't just a cause or an abstraction. It meant becoming a traitor, turning against the established authority, risking life, property, and honor to go against the beliefs of the majority. Now he understood why Sally Crewe had been afraid of him when he first came to the house with Peterson in tow. She'd thought him on the British side, and Peterson was a clear implication of her sympathies with the patriots. Only . . . Robert had said that Sally was a Tory. It didn't add up, unless . . .

"She's a double agent, isn't she?"

Robert stopped dead in his tracks. His face went as white as his cravat, but he shook his head. "I don't know what you mean, sir."

"Forget it, Robert. You lie worse than I do. And you talk too much. You trust too much."

Robert flushed to the roots of his hair. "I—"

"Don't worry. I won't betray you or your sister. That's not why I'm here."

"Thank you!" said Robert, gripping his arm with such relief in his eyes that Noel had to look away. "Ever since Papa died, there's been no handling her. She thinks she's up to the mark, but she's green when it comes to politics. And I can't protect her because she won't let me."

"No, I guess not." Noel looked into the boy's worried eyes. "As for this mysterious plot that's hatching in town, is my brother involved in it?"

"I'm sure of it! That is, he always seems to know what's going on. He's like a cat with his whiskers in every corner. I avoid him when I can because it's as though he can read my mind."

Startled, Noel gripped Robert's shoulder. "Nonsense."

"Well, yes, but he's awfully sharp and he always seems to know what you're going to do before you do it. You know what I mean."

"I do indeed," said Noel softly. Leon's telepathy enabled him to manipulate minds. He could convince people that they'd known him forever. He could make them do what he wanted. Noel, on the other hand, had no such ability. He was always scrambling to gain trust and having to dodge suspicion.

"Here's where he lodges," said Robert, halting by a trim house with green shutters. Its boxwood hedge glittered with melting ice. A yellow tabby cat sat on the front steps and stared at them coldly.

Noel stared up at the house. "On the third floor?"

"Yes. I'd better get home. Sally will be anxious about me. And she may need help."

Noel shook hands with him. "Thanks for your help, Robert. If anything goes wrong, I'll help out."

"Oh! Yes, thank you," said Robert, nodding at the greeting of some men who passed by. "But we can surely manage. Good-bye!"

Robert darted off up the street with his coattails flying.

Noel watched him, thankful that he didn't have to deal with the problems of the Crewe family. For once his task seemed simple. All he had to do was wait for Leon in his room. If by some miracle history hadn't been changed, there was nothing to delay recall.

He shifted his hand in his pocket, where his LOC still glowed warmly around his burned finger. The discomfort of that had grown past his ability to hide it, and he was glad Robert was finally gone.

"LOC, deactivate," he murmured, and it shut down.

Pulling his hand from his pocket, he hesitated a moment, then walked up the steps. He opened the door without knocking and entered. The interior of the house was warm, stuffy, and dark. It smelled of beeswax, tobacco, lavender, and cooked cabbage. A maid in an apron and mobcap crouched on her hands and knees, scrubbing the floor.

"Mind you get none of that mud on my clean floor, Lieutenant," she said sharply but gave him a broad wink.

Knowing exactly how Leon would react, Noel said nothing as he passed her, but he gave her backside a roguish pinch that left her giggling. He went up the stairs, carrying his filthy shoes in his hand. On the landing a longcase clock ticked solemnly.

Time passing . . . but right now things seemed to be going in his favor. He entered Leon's room without anyone challenging him and shut the door with a sag of relief. Wiping the nervous perspiration from his face, he glanced around at the furnishings. The ashes had been swept up from the hearth, and the room was cold. There was a narrow rope bed, a washstand with a jug and basin of plain porcelain, a small table containing a wig stand and a pair of silver-backed brushes. Digging through the chest, Noel found a pair of new top boots, some buckskin breeches, clean linen, and a mulberry-hued coat that still had the tailor's bill pinned to it. Everything fit well enough, and although once Noel would have rather died than wear Leon's clothes, now he was simply grateful to find them.

Dressed and cleaned up, he pulled out his empty pistol and loaded it with the powder and shot he found along with Leon's spare uniform. There was a thin book lying on the bed's pillow. Bound in much-worn calf, with a ribbon for the marker, it was a collection of poetry. Leon had written his name on the flyleaf, along with the date he'd purchased the volume.

Holding the little book, Noel suddenly felt a pang inside. In that instant he could imagine his duplicate walking into a bookshop and buying the secondhand book of poems with a sense of accomplishment. He could imagine Leon's pride in writing his name on the page, in owning *something*, in having a possession.

Had Leon ever owned anything before? Had Leon ever felt settled somewhere? Found a home for himself? Made friends? Become a part of a community?

How could he? Leon was a freak, the result of an accident in the time stream. His duplication was against nature. He couldn't be allowed to continue as he was, for he was supposed to exist as a part of Noel.

Leon had often said he wanted to belong somewhere. Much of his hatred of Noel stemmed from the frustration of being yanked from place to place as Noel moved through the time stream.

No, Leon could never make a life for himself. Could never have a family. Could never belong.

And for the first time, Noel realized the loneliness Leon must feel. These meager possessions were pathetic in how well they were cared for, in how proud Leon was of them.

He put the book down, aghast at what he'd perceived. Leon was a monster, but the problem was he knew it and wanted to be something else.

"Impossible," whispered Noel.

Leon would never change. Even supposing he had lived in this time for weeks or months and had restrained himself from changing history, or from trying to destroy the future, even supposing that he hoped to blend in here apart and undiscovered by Noel, he could not be allowed to continue. The laws of nature would not permit Noel and Leon to remain split. Noel had reluctantly accepted the fact that he must have Leon's darkness back inside himself. Leon would never consent to become a part of Noel's personality again.

Noel wandered back across the room. Sympathy or not, it was a trap he laid here. Noel sighed and, with his pistol in his hand, settled himself to wait for his twin's arrival.

CHAPTER 7

Galloping down a dirt road at dusk, the cold air snapping in his ears, Leon grinned to himself with satisfaction. The news he'd managed to gather on today's scouting trip would delight Major Burton. He'd been to watch practice troop maneuvers, skirting Valley Forge and finding it easy to blank the sentries' stupid minds and slip past. Several sketches in his pocket would testify that Washington's ragtag forces had indeed learned to march and drill during the winter. Yes, the major would be very pleased with the wealth of information he had to offer. And if his scheme to assassinate Washington succeeded, Leon was counting on a promotion.

Not that Burton knew about Leon's plans. The Brit was old-fashioned, conservative, and stodgy when it came to new ideas. He believed in a gentleman's code, stupidly adhered to honor, and would have been horrified at the thought of cold-blooded murder. Leon, of course, knew it was the perfect solution to this whole conflict. The colonies all revered George Washington far beyond his abilities. He had never formally trained as a military leader. His youthful service in the Virginia regiment during the French and Indian War had been full of error and stupidity. But here he was, this charismatic leader. Without him, the whole revolt would fold. With him, England would lose this country and all its potential.

Of course Leon could not tell Burton that. He had learned over the past few weeks to resist small temptations to tamper with the path of history. No, he intended to bide his time and make the big strike. Tomorrow night, Washington's fate would be in his hands and he—

Without warning a net of darkness surrounded him, blacking out the sky and shadowy trees. His horse neighed in fright and plunged to a rearing halt, nearly pitching Leon from the saddle.

"Noel?" he gasped, dragging on the reins in an effort to control his mount.

A ghostly figure hovered before him, and his snorting horse tried to back away from it.

"Hold still, damn you!" shouted Leon. But it was all bravado. As soon as he had the horse's attention, he whirled it around and spurred it cruelly.

But although the horse gathered itself, trembling and snorting, it did not bolt. The apparition appeared before them again, and again, no matter which way Leon turned. Enraged by its interference, he gathered the strength of his mind and hurled it at the thing.

The force, kinetic and alien, scattered briefly beneath his mental blow, then regathered itself. It deflected his next attack. Short of breath, Leon froze in place and watched the thing with new wariness. Whatever it was, it possessed more strength than he had. He would not attack it again until he understood how to defeat it.

"I am Qwip," said the image to his mind.

"So?" replied Leon with a sneer. "Get out of my way."

"I deliver a warning."

Leon's wariness increased. "What is it?"

"Noel waits for you."

Rage swept through Leon. This was some kind of new trick. He should have known. "I knew it was you!" he said in a fury. "Get away! Leave me be!"

"I am not Noel," said the image. "I am Qwip."

"And I don't care. I'll hear no message from *him*."

"No message is delivered. I have warned you."

"Why?"

"That is not important."

"No," admitted Leon craftily. He decided that perhaps this thing wasn't from Noel after all. Who then? Had the anarchists of Noel's time figured out how to access the time stream? It was an intriguing possibility.

"I am not of Noel's time," said the image. "I am Qwip."

"Yeah, like I care," muttered Leon. "You're saying that Noel is here?"

"He waits for you."

Leon's fist slammed against the pommel of his saddle. "Why can't he leave me alone? I thought he'd returned to the future that's so damned precious to him. Why must he interfere?"

"He is trapped like yourself. You remain linked."

"That's crazy," said Leon with another sneer. "I've been here for nearly three months. If we were still linked, he would have shown up immediately. You're trying to trick me."

"Accept the warning or reject it as you please," said the image tonelessly.

"Nothing comes for free," said Leon. "What do you want in exchange?"

Qwip laughed, and it was a hollow, eerie sound that made the hairs rise on the back of Leon's neck. There was little enough in this world that could frighten him, but suddenly he felt unnaturally cold and vulnerable.

Qwip surged at him. So fast did it move, Leon barely had time to tense himself against the attack. Qwip's strength hit him like a blow, and with a hoarse cry Leon tumbled off his horse. The animal bolted down the road, but Leon was too busy grappling with the thing that had seized him. There was no physical body to fight, no corporeal form to resist. All was mental energy, as slippery and elusive as the ether, yet the pressure of it made him scream. He felt as though his skull would crack, and no matter how much he struggled, he could not cast this thing away.

"No!" he screamed, rolling over and over. The silver gorget of his rank clanged against a pebble in the road, and he writhed madly. The pressure continued to mount, until his eyeballs felt as though they would explode. His tongue projected from his mouth, his skin felt as though it were being shredded from his bones, and he was racked with muscle spasms. He uttered mindless screams.

Then, with a suddenness that silenced him, it was in.

He could feel the alien coldness of it slithering around in his mind, handling his thoughts, sifting through his memories and knowledge. It gripped him harshly and he would have screamed had he still possessed breath.

The horror, the fear . . . *No, no, no*, screamed his mind. But it held him in a force he could not escape.

"Now," whispered Qwip to him, "you will act as I wish you to."

"No," sobbed Leon. "*No!*"

Qwip hurt him, and the pain was so great he lost consciousness. When Qwip let his mind recover, he found himself curled in a small ball upon the frozen ground, whimpering.

"Enough," said Qwip. "I can make it worse if I choose."

Closing his eyes, Leon rocked himself from side to side and fought no more against the creature.

"Now," whispered Qwip as though licking at his mind, "go to Noel."

CHAPTER 8

Noel awakened from an uneasy doze with a start and looked around wildly. For an instant he did not recognize his surroundings. Then the ordinary shapes of bed and table amid the twilight shadows reassured him. He sank back in his chair and ran his hands through his hair. His body was still trembling, and he was covered with a light film of perspiration despite the chilliness of the room. He knew he'd had a nightmare, but he couldn't remember any of it. He was glad.

Restless, he stood up and paced around the room. He was starving. It was getting late, and he'd lost his patience. When was Leon going to show up?

He thought over the duties of an army officer. Leon could be anywhere. He might have been sent off on a mission, providing he would consent to take orders from anyone. Or he might be down at the tavern carousing with his friends.

Noel sighed. He should have known his plan was too simplistic to work. Hours were passing, and he was no closer to getting his hands on his duplicate than when he'd started. Besides, since he'd been stupid enough to fall asleep, Leon could have come to the house, sensed his presence, and left.

"Damn!" said Noel.

His sense of unease increased. He listened at the door but heard nothing beyond the ordinary sounds of a household. Yet something was wrong. He felt restless, too uneasy to linger in this room. It had begun to feel like a trap to him, too small, too dark.

Picking up his pistol, he took a cloak of Leon's, and a hat that did not quite fit, and eased open the door. The stairs beyond the landing were quite dark. He made his way down them cautiously, feeling each step, and let himself out the side door.

As he was crossing the garden, however, he saw a furtive shadow move among the shrubbery. A second later, a lean silhouette faced him by the starlight, one that he would recognize anywhere.

Noel froze, mentally kicking himself for not waiting just a few minutes more. When was he ever going to learn more patience?

Still, the mistake had been made. There was no going back now.

"Leon," he said quietly.

"Noel," came the reply.

Leon's voice was hoarse and oddly breathless. Since Noel was aware of the intense hatred Leon felt for him, he was hardly surprised that his duplicate sounded under a strain. He made a surreptitious move for the pistol in his pocket and heard the sound of a gun hammer being pulled back.

"Don't," said Leon.

Noel grimaced to himself. "I should have known I couldn't surprise you."

"No, you are always predictable, at least where I am concerned. I blame you for this. Why didn't you stay away?"

"I'm not here by choice," said Noel.

Leon gave a choking laugh. "Three months of life . . . the sweetness of it. Just when I began to hope, you come to tell me it was all just a great cosmic joke at my expense. Did you laugh, Noel? I hope you laughed."

The bitterness in Leon's voice was rawer than Noel had ever heard it. He thought of the little book and the silver-backed brushes and felt the stirrings of compassion.

"Why?" asked Leon. "*Why?* I didn't tamper this time. I swear I didn't. I've stolen nothing, seduced few—"

"Don't," said Noel harshly, unable to bear the appeal.

A short span of silence stretched between them. Then Leon said, "This is hard to believe. You aren't protesting your innocence or giving me a lecture on the evils of my ways."

"Would it do any good?" asked Noel wearily. "You have to go back with me."

"Oh, yes, at last here it is. I wondered when you would get to the speech. Now tell me, brother dear, what is the cataclysm awaiting the world—excuse me—the *future* world this time? And exactly how is it my fault?"

"I don't know what you've done," said Noel. "Nothing that I can determine."

Leon gave a muted, mocking whistle.

"That doesn't change anything!" said Noel desperately.

"I thought I always changed things. That's your constant accusation."

"The rip in the time stream is still out there. We were joined for a moment, but it didn't hold."

"Because we're not one being, as you'd like to believe. I can't imagine why you're so desperate to have me, since you despise me."

"I don't—"

"I'm a cockroach to you!" shouted Leon.

"That isn't true."

"Isn't it?" said Leon with a jeer. "And what's this new note I hear in your voice, brother dear? Pity? Hah! I want none of that, thank you."

"What do you want?" asked Noel quietly.

Leon tensed. The hatred rolling off him was palpable, even in the shadows. "Yes, mock me. Pretend you don't know. As though I haven't pleaded with you a dozen times, begging you heart and soul to let me live."

"No," said Noel in puzzlement. "There's something different about you this time. Something else you want."

"I want a promotion from my commanding officer," said Leon raggedly. "Don't laugh."

"I'm not laughing."

"I'm really trying this time."

"So it seems."

"I want a real life. I have friends this time, a job, a place in this community. I've had time to become a part of it. I want to stay."

Noel heard the aching sincerity in his voice and regretted it. "You know it isn't possible."

"But I've proven myself. I haven't tampered, haven't used my telepathy to do harm."

"Perhaps."

"You doubt my word?"

Noel said nothing.

"Why did you wait so long?" demanded Leon. "Why did you let me think I had a chance—"

"It wasn't my doing—"

"It never is," said Leon bitterly. "How can you always come up with this sanctimonious drivel?"

Keeping a wary eye on the pistol in Leon's hand, Noel changed the subject swiftly. "Where did you materialize?" he asked. "At the battle of—"

"I don't want to discuss that," said Leon sharply.

"But it's important. I landed right in the middle of a battle and had to run for my life from British soldiers."

Leon chuckled so softly it was like hearing a ghost laugh. "I wish I had seen that."

"You should have. I expected you to be there."

"Nonsense!" said Leon. "Don't tell me that you've been here for three months too. Your LOC would have recalled you long ago."

Noel said nothing.

Leon drew in a sharp breath. "You still have it, don't you?"

Noel thought back to their last encounter in Restoration London, when they'd fought to the bitter end and Leon had destroyed his own LOC, thus trapping them both in a new time loop. The old anger returned, and he took an involuntary step forward.

Leon raised the pistol. "Careful."

"You idiot," said Noel through his teeth. "When you destroyed your LOC, you trapped us both. I hope that's satisfied you."

"I was perfectly satisfied until you came here."

Noel looked at him. "You do realize that in a few more months the tide of this war will turn in the colonials' favor? Do you plan to stay in the army and return to England? What if you're killed in battle?"

"Worried?" retorted Leon.

"Anytime you're on the scene, I'm worried," said Noel with equal sharpness.

"Are you saying that your LOC no longer functions?"

"Why are you so concerned with my LOC?" asked Noel with fresh puzzlement. "You can't steal it. You know it won't work for you. Besides, how do you think I got here without it?"

"How did *I* get here?"

"I told you. I materialized on the battlefield. That's how you came along. I'm sure that's how you acquired a uniform."

"Full of theories, aren't you?"

"Your pattern is consistent."

"And you're full of lies."

Noel sighed. "Yes, you think so. I'm always lying to you, betraying you, trying to destroy you. You're suffering from a persecution complex."

"How's your metabolism this trip?" asked Leon angrily. "A little more normal? Will you survive a lead ball in your chest?"

Noel tensed. Leon was unpredictable and half-crazy. He might just shoot.

"Don't look so worried," said Leon. "I'm not ready to shoot you yet. First of all, I'd have to explain you."

"Oh, I'm your brother and I'm here to take you back to England at the request of our father," said Noel blithely. "And you're illegitimate, by the way."

Leon snorted. "Nice touch."

"I thought so."

"I won't sell my commission."

"You must. Especially when I've explained matters to your commanding officer."

"Burton won't believe your tale."

"But I'm obviously your twin," said Noel reasonably. "No one can doubt our relationship."

"Who says anyone is going to meet you?"

"But I've met so many of your acquaintances already."

Leon stiffened. "Who, damn you? Who?"

"Let's see. The Crewes and—"

"Sally Crewe?"

Surprised by the alarm in Leon's voice, Noel stared at him. "Yes."

"How the hell did you—never mind!"

"Oh, I know all about her," said Noel cheerfully, ready to goad any weak point he could find. "Tell me, is this little romance with the major all in her mind, or does Burton feel the same way about her?"

"You devil—"

"What does it matter if I've met her?" asked Noel blankly.

"Nothing!" said Leon, but with too much vehemence.

"I just spoke with her briefly at—"

"I said to forget it. It doesn't matter," snapped Leon.

Noel could tell that it did. "She's kind of snooty," he remarked. "But everything else about her is spectacular."

"Just shut up."

"Why?"

"Shut up!"

Noel stared at him in dawning realization. "You *like* her!" he said in amazement. "My God, you've got it for your commander's girlfriend!"

"Why don't you shout it across the town square?" growled Leon. "I told you to shut up about it."

"But why?" asked Noel, laughing. "Leon in love? I didn't think you could feel anything but greed and hatred. Perhaps you're becoming human after all."

Leon glared at him. "I could shoot you for that," he said in a low, furious voice. "I can't right now, but if it weren't for—" He broke off, breathing hard, then continued raggedly. "The moment will come when you'll regret making fun of me."

"But I'm not—"

"Enough!" He gestured with the pistol. "It's too exposed out here. Anyone from the house could see us. Go that way, behind the house."

Holding his hands where Leon could see them, Noel turned slowly and walked across the garden. His footsteps crunched on the frost, and the air was so cold it hurt to breathe it. His back felt exposed. There was a spot just beneath his left shoulder blade that itched with anticipation, but so far Leon hadn't shot him. Perhaps Leon had lost his nerve again. But Noel knew he couldn't count on that.

Past the garden wall there was a sort of common field, with woods beyond. Noel stopped, still holding up his hands.

"Now where?" he asked.

He heard the quick scrape of Leon's boots behind him and started to turn, but he was too late.

The hard pistol butt crashed into his head. With a grunt, Noel pitched forward on his face and knew no more.

Noel awakened to the unpleasant sensation of being dragged by one heel across some cold and very lumpy ground. His head was muzzy and throbbing, but after a few moments his wits cleared. He raised his head and saw that he was indeed being dragged, by Leon.

His duplicate was taking him across the field behind the town for some inexplicable reason, to bury him perhaps. But worse than that was the sound Leon was making, a mewing kind of mindless noise over and over in his throat. It was the sound of something deranged, something wild. It made Noel's skin crawl.

He thought about calling out to his duplicate, but a sense of caution held him silent. They were perhaps twenty yards from the trees, and instinct warned Noel against letting himself be dragged there.

He didn't try to reason it out. At the first opportunity he grabbed a root sticking out of the frozen ground and held tight. Leon halted, still moaning, and turned slowly. He tugged at Noel's foot.

Noel arched his back and kicked Leon in the side with his other foot. Leon went staggering, and Noel scrambled to his feet.

"Stop!" said Leon and drew his pistol. "I—you—I—"

He seemed unable to complete his sentence, but even as he struggled to aim the weapon Noel tackled him to the ground, struggling all the while until he managed to wrest the pistol away. Leon thrashed and cried out beneath him like something demented. It seemed that he did not fight Noel as much as himself.

Either way, he was dangerous. Noel struck him and knocked him out cold. Even so, it was a long moment before Leon's unconscious body stopped jerking and twitching.

Frowning in puzzlement at this strange behavior, Noel knelt on the ground and examined him. Leon's skin was feverishly hot to the touch. His heart, located on the right side of his chest, pounded much too hard and fast. It was as though his body was being driven to act, even when it couldn't. Noel had never seen Leon ill, other than the one time Leon had taken a pirate's knife meant for him, and this sudden collapse worried him. Leon had always felt Noel's pain and discomfort through the link between them, but the reverse was not usually true. Still, as Noel wrapped his fingers around Leon's bared wrist to check his pulse a second time, the oddest feeling ran through him. It was similar to receiving a shock of static electricity, not painful but disorienting in a small way. He released Leon's wrist, and his fingers tingled. Flexing them, he put on his gloves just to be safe. Leon had drawn energy from him before, and he didn't want to be drained this time.

Still breathing hard from the struggle, Noel shook his head to clear it and slung Leon over his shoulder. Staggering some under his duplicate's weight, he headed for the cover of the woods.

This was his chance, and he didn't intend to lose it.

As soon as he'd stumbled several yards into the woods, far enough into the undergrowth where he couldn't be seen from the houses at the edge of town, Noel slid Leon off his shoulder and leaned against a tree to catch his breath. Starlight overhead glittered through the skeletal treetops. To his left he heard an owl hoot and the furtive rustle of some animal. The primitive part of his brain cortex shivered with instinctive alarm, but Noel told himself to get on with it.

Crouching beside his unconscious duplicate, Noel pulled off his left glove. "LOC, activate."

At once a soft blue light illuminated the spot. The signet ring shimmered and started to change shape, then held steady. Noel felt encouraged; perhaps the LOC was succeeding in working internal repairs.

Leon began to twitch and make little snorting sounds. He would wake up soon.

Noel gripped his wrist. "LOC," he said urgently, "scan to the time portal. Is the time stream clear?"

"Affirmative."

"Has history been altered?"

"Negative."

"Any anomalies in time?"

"Negative."

"Do you have contact with the portal?"

"Affirmative."

Noel swallowed, hope and excitement rising in him. He would like to know the futures of Robert and Sally Crewe, but he could always research that in the Institute library when he got back. "Has—has previous recall imbalance been corrected?"

"Negative."

"Can you compensate?"

"I am programmed to recall with two LOCs."

"Yes, I know, but I'm overriding that programming sequence now. I have physical contact with Leon. Can you recall us both?"

"Override . . . completed," said the LOC.

Noel took a deep breath. "Initiate recall sequence . . . now."

"Affirmative. Recall commencing."

The peculiar sensation of dissolving enveloped Noel. He felt Leon's arm jerk in his grasp, but he held on more tightly. It was going to work. This time it had to work.

The piercing whine of feedback suddenly deafened him. Light flashed around him with such brilliance he was momentarily blinded. Blinking, his eyes streaming with tears, he found himself buffeted by an electrical backlash that made his hair stand on end. His whole body felt as though little things were crawling across it. The whine grew louder and more piercing until his eardrums ached from it. The LOC on his finger grew blazing hot on the burns he'd already suffered.

Through his own outcry, he could hear Leon screaming. Then the LOC began to intone, "Warning. Sequence cannot be completed. Warning. Sequence cannot be completed. Warning—"

"Stop!" yelled Noel. "Cancel recall sequence!"

He smelled something burning, whether flesh or circuitry he could not tell. There was an explosion, and smoke, and he found himself hurled backward. He struck a tree hard and collapsed on the ground, dazed and shaken.

The LOC was still flashing on his finger, almost incandescent with heat. "Overload," it said shrilly. "Overload!"

"Deactivate!" he ordered.

The light vanished, and with it the piercing whine. Ringing silence followed. His eardrums ached, and despite the darkness he still had purple spots dancing in front of his eyes. The pain in his hand was incredible, the flesh weeping and raw. Crouched there, Noel rocked himself in misery. He could hear Leon whimpering at a distance, but he couldn't see him in the darkness.

What had gone wrong?

Right then he didn't care. He was too full of disappointment and pain. At that moment he could have overcome his conditioning and thrown the LOC away forever, but there was no hope of pulling the ring off his burned finger. The very thought of trying made him break out in a cold sweat.

Leon's scream jerked him from his daze. He scrambled unsteadily to his feet and swayed, swearing to keep from crying.

"Leon?" his voice came out as a croak.

He staggered forward, bumping into trees and catching limbs in his face. But Leon wasn't far, and Noel tripped over him. He landed on his knees with a gasp.

Leon was writhing madly, tossing himself about and tearing at the ground with his hands. "Get it *out*! Get it out!" he screamed.

"Quiet!" snapped Noel. He inadvertently bumped his injured hand and winced. "We've made enough noise already."

Dogs were barking. Several lights had appeared in windows. Some brave souls would venture out soon to investigate.

Noel put his hand on Leon's shoulder and tried to press him down. "Be still, damn you."

"Get it out. Get it out! Get it out!" Leon's entire body shuddered, and he jerked and screamed in mindless agony.

Noel gripped his jaw and tried to hold him. "Stop it. You've got to be quiet."

But as before the touch of Leon's skin gave him the oddest sensation. He felt as though he'd touched something alien. He jerked back and frowned as Leon panted and convulsed. Instinctively Noel moved away. There was something wrong, something beyond mere injury.

Fear caught him in the throat, and he almost ran. But anger at his own cowardice held him there. If he abandoned Leon now, he might never find him again.

"Leon," he said. "Leon!"

His duplicate reared up to a sitting position. "Stop!" he said, throwing himself back, then sitting up again. With one fist he began to hit himself in the chest, in the throat, in the face. "Stop!"

Noel stared at him. Leon had gone completely mad. Whatever hadn't worked correctly in the recall attempt must have snapped his reason.

Horrified, Noel said, "Leon—"

With a choked cry, Leon hurled himself bodily at Noel, flailing wildly with fists that struck himself as much as they hit Noel. He fought back, although he was hampered by his injuries. His burned hand twisted beneath him as Leon wrestled him down, and the resulting agony drove Noel's temper high.

"Get off me!" he snarled, and hit Leon in the solar plexus hard enough to double him up. Coughing and sobbing, Leon fell onto his side and drew up his knees. Noel hit him again, and knocked him unconscious.

Between his throbbing hand and his throbbing head, Noel felt himself done for. But he could hear people talking in the distance. Torches had been lit. They were working up the courage to investigate. If the townspeople dared not, then the soldiers would.

Noel couldn't risk discovery, not like this. Leon was already accepted by the British as one of their own. When he woke up, Leon would tell them anything to keep Noel away. Noel didn't intend to be locked up, shot, or hanged.

If he was going to run for it, he'd better do it now.

Groaning under his breath, he forced himself to his knees, then to his feet. A little voice deep inside him kept urging him to abandon Leon and save himself, but that wasn't what he had come here for.

And if the LOC was damaged forever?

Noel shook his head, angry and stubborn.

You're trapped here. Save yourself. Get away and start a life.

Noel lifted his face to the sky. "No," he said aloud. "I won't give up yet."

Drawing on the last reserves of his strength, he pulled Leon over his shoulder in a fireman's lift and staggered deeper into the woods with him.

CHAPTER 9

He hid, pressed behind a rotting log, while a handful of grumbling soldiers searched the fringes of the woods.

"Nothing here, Corporal!"

"All right. All right. Come forth, then. Damned colonials and their fancies."

"Seeing ghosts they are."

Another man spat. "Or hearing Indians after their scalps."

"Or thinking the end of the world is come. Gawd above, did you ever hear the like?"

They trooped off, grumbling and complaining, back to their ale and their warm fire.

Gradually the lights went out in the windows, and things settled down. The woods remained as silent as the grave around Noel, however. He forced himself to wait another hour, shivering with cold and shock, before he finally crept out of hiding.

His priority was to find shelter, a sanctuary where he and Leon would not be discovered or disturbed.

By the time he reached the back garden of Mr. Smyth's house, he had rejected Leon's quarters. They were close and tempting, but it was too risky to venture into the house, and he could never feel safe there. He knew of nowhere in town where they would not be discovered, especially once Leon awoke and began to protest.

Moving as quietly as he could, Noel stole into the stable and saddled a horse. He was jumpy and tense, expecting discovery at any moment. Outside, a cat squalled from a fence. Someone opened a window and flung a shoe at it. Silence closed in again.

Still hardly daring to breathe, Noel led the horse outside. It shied when he slung Leon across it, but Noel managed to climb on. Pulling his hat low, he eased the horse into the alley shadows, walking slowly to keep the hoofbeats quiet. In his heart he wanted to run, but he dared not be that foolish.

There was a sentry at the bridge, his musket on his shoulder and a lantern at his feet.

Noel watched from afar for a moment, but crossing the bridge was impossible. He eased into the trees bordering the river and followed its course until he was well away from town. When he reached a spot where the bank looked fairly low, he urged his mount to plunge in.

The shock of the icy water robbed him of breath. The river was deep and swollen; within seconds the horse had lost his footing and was swimming. Noel felt himself floating off the saddle. He clung tightly to the pommel and kept a strong grip on Leon's coat, holding his duplicate's head out of the water to prevent him from drowning.

He'd feared the water would revive Leon, but it didn't. By the time the horse reached the opposite bank and lunged out, shaking itself violently, Noel was completely numb. His boots were full of freezing water. He couldn't feel his toes. His teeth chattered uncontrollably. The night air had been bitterly cold before; now it was knife-sharp. His wet clothes clung to his body like sheets of ice. He was so cold, he couldn't think, couldn't move. His fingers felt frozen to the reins or he would probably have dropped them.

Common sense said he should dismount and build a fire. He had to warm himself quickly before hypothermia got him.

But he feared if he got off his horse, he'd never be able to get on again. His senses were failing him. He caught himself drooping low over his horse's neck. Deliberately he braced his injured hand on Leon's back and pushed with all his might.

The agony drove away the mists and sharpened his mind once again. He kicked the horse forward into a trot, then a canter. Reeling in the saddle, he pressed his injured hand each time he felt himself slipping toward unconsciousness. His chest was like ice. It hurt to breathe. And he was so very cold.

By the time he reached Sally Crewe's lane, he was nearly gone.

Leon lay so still across the horse that he feared his duplicate had drowned. The horse, eager for a barn, pricked its ears and hurried until it reached the picket fence and stopped.

A startled dog let out a single yelp from behind the house. An upstairs shutter opened cautiously, and a voice called out gruffly, "Who's there?"

Noel felt himself sway in the saddle. "Robert," he whispered. He gathered himself and made it louder. "Robert."

A light shone out. "Who is it, I said?" called Robert.

"K-Kedran."

The shutters banged wide. "Mr. Kedran?" called Robert, leaning out in his nightshirt. The tassel on his nightcap swept across his shoulder. "What's amiss?" Before Noel could answer, he popped back inside and Noel could hear him talking to someone else. "Yes, it's Mr. Kedran. The lieutenant's brother from England. You remember what I told you." He leaned out again. "Mr. Kedran?"

Noel tried to stop his teeth from chattering long enough to answer. "Brought more trouble. Sorry."

"Wait."

Robert disappeared, only to fling open the front door moments later. He had tucked his nightshirt into a pair of breeches and he held a lantern in his hand.

"Jupiter!" he said at the gate. "You're wet through."

Noel nodded, still wracked with shivering. "River."

"Did you swim it? But why? And who is that with you? Another—"

"Robert?" came Sally's cool, imperious voice. A moment later she appeared in the lighted doorway. She was wearing a dressing gown of rosebud pink and a sleeping cap. Her golden hair lay across her shoulder in a braid. Seeing her illuminated in the candlelight thus, her skin luminescent, her blue eyes brighter than jewels, Noel felt something catch inside him. He understood all too well why she had a major interested in her, why Leon had lost his heart—crippled though it was—to her, why she was at the center of intrigue in this tiny Pennsylvania community. She was the most beautiful creature he had ever seen.

"Do not stand there with the night air blowing us to our deaths with cold," she scolded. "Is he drunk? What does he want at this late hour?"

"I told you it was Mr. Kedran," said Robert, taking the reins from Noel's shaking hands. "He's been in the river and is about to perish of cold. It looks like he's found another injured man."

Sally drew up a shawl around her shoulders and walked outside. "We are not a hospital, Mr. Kedran. I wonder you are not weary of playing good Samaritan."

All he wanted from her was warmth and shelter. Her cool hostility was more than he could cope with. "N-need . . . Could I stay in your b-barn?"

"Why, it's Lieutenant Nardek!" exclaimed Robert. "Whatever's happened to him, sir?"

Sally looked alarmed. "This is trouble indeed that you bring us. I tell you we want none of it. Go elsewhere, if you please."

"Oh, Sally," said Robert in protest, "that's too harsh. 'Pon my soul, the man's freezing."

If he had not been so cold, so spent, Noel would have ridden all night rather than ask her for anything. But if Leon did not die, he thought he must. "P-please," he whispered.

She said something else and Robert spoke, but things started spinning and Noel could no longer make out their words. He felt himself going, trying to grip the saddle in an effort to hang on, and went crashing to the ground.

The impact roused him, but only halfway. Someone pulled him up. He saw Robert's face wavering over him and tried to grip the boy's shirt.

"Leon," he gasped out. "L-lock him up. Can't—"

And he was gone.

The smell of chicken broth roused him. Noel dragged his eyes open with a struggle and found himself in a narrow bed with a stack of heavy quilts pinning him down. A fire roared on the hearth, casting ruddy light about the room, and Sally was leaning down to set a tray on a little bedside table. To his disappointment she had exchanged the dressing gown for the blue wool dress he'd seen earlier in the day. Her hair was still loose and soft on her shoulders. He pulled his good hand free of the covers, wanting to touch it.

She turned. "Ah, so you're awake again. Good. Drink some of this."

"I—"

"Don't talk just yet. Swallow the broth first."

She propped another pillow behind him and held a cup to his lips. He tried to take it from her, but he was shivering so violently he nearly spilled the broth.

"I'll hold it. You drink," she said.

He sipped at the warmth broth, found it delicious, and gulped like a starving man.

"Gently, sir," she said, but more kindly than before. "You act as though you've gone without your dinner. Let that warm you and we'll see about more in a moment."

She set the empty cup down, and Noel let his head sink back in the pillow. Already the broth was doing its stuff, warming his core and spreading outward. He turned his head to watch her, and saw Leon lying in a similar bed on the other side of the small room.

"He's here?" said Noel in surprise. "I—"

"Hush," she commanded, wringing out a cloth and laying it across Leon's forehead. "You told us to lock him up, as though he were bound for the pillory."

"Yes—"

"Nonsense. The lieutenant is very ill. And you will be too if you are not quiet." She gave him a severe look. "I'm out of patience with you, coming here like this, when I've got quite enough on my hands already."

"Peterson—"

Her busy hands stilled and she looked away. "I'm afraid he's dead."

"Oh."

"We'll bury him tomorrow when the ground has softened again. It'll be as Christian and as decent as we can make it. If only it had happened sooner, then no one in town need have known he was ever here."

Noel frowned. "Poor devil."

"Do not criticize," she said angrily. "I am doing the best I can."

"Are you?"

"Major Burton was here for dinner tonight, and me with a traitor lying upstairs. It was enough to drive me mad. I tried to cry off and cancel the invitation, but Dr. Selincourt couldn't run fast enough back to town with his suspicions, and now—and now—"

A tremor entered her voice and she sat staring into space while her fingers pleated knots in her dress.

"And now you're suspect," said Noel. "Because I brought him here. I shouldn't have interfered, but two against one was unfair. And he died anyway. I'm sorry."

Her lips started to tremble. "I thought the major truly cared—but it's only been a flirtation, a trifle to him. He said—" With difficulty she bit back the rest of her sentence. "It doesn't matter."

"Yes, it does," said Noel. Her distress was so strong he couldn't help but feel sorry for her. "I know I'm a stranger, but Robert trusts me. You can too."

She tossed her head. "And I suppose for no other reason than your fine gray eyes?"

Then she blushed at what she had said.

Noel had to grin a little. "Why not? No, I really wouldn't betray you. And you are in trouble, aren't you, Miss Crewe?"

Her eyes went to his and she looked as though she would confide in him, then she drew back and tightened her mouth. "It is only a—a misunderstanding. It will clear up by and by. If—if only you hadn't come, sir, now of all times! I fear he may decide to have the house watched, and with the ball already planned, I—" She gave her head a little shake. "Forgive me. I can be making little sense. I am not myself."

"I wish you'd tell me what really happened."

"You could not help me, sir. I would rather hear what has occurred between you and the lieutenant."

Noel went off into a fit of violent coughing that left him spent for breath.

"There, your lungs are affected already. I shan't ask why you didn't take the bridge. It's plain you have tried to kidnap Lieutenant Nardek."

"Is it now?" said Noel with annoyance.

"Oh, Robert told me your tale. Only no one could believe such poppycock."

"I must take him home."

"Honorable men bearing urgent messages from home would go to the lieutenant's commanding officer, which you did not."

"No?"

"No," she said coolly. "I asked the major this evening, and he was completely taken by surprise. He said as far as he knew the lieutenant's only brother was dead."

Noel narrowed his eyes. "Not quite."

"Well, if you've been cast off by your family, I suppose they might prefer to think you dead," she said matter-of-factly.

"I'm not a black sheep!"

"Keep quiet. You will bring on another coughing fit if you yell."

Noel turned his head away from her, fuming. If she was trying to distract him from her problems, she'd succeeded. He could care less what trouble she was in.

"Robert said that you've hurt your hand. Let me see it, please."

"It's fine," said Noel.

"I doubt that."

He glared at her. "Thanks, but it's fine."

"Are you a liar as well as a scoundrel and a kidnapper? Give me your hand." She met his gaze and a hint of a smile quivered suddenly at the corner of her mouth. "Come, sir. Don't be such a baby about it. I am sure it does need attention."

Wincing, he reluctantly drew his left hand from beneath the covers.

She gasped when she saw it. "This is very badly burned. How came you by such an injury? Robert said the two of you must have been in a fight, but I do not think so. And this ring must have you in agony."

"Don't touch it!" said Noel so sharply he startled her.

She stared at him, her blue eyes very wide.

By candlelight his hand looked terrible. Streaked with black, the skin across the back and the palm was red and puffy. His fingers were a blistered mess. Seeing it clearly for the first time made it hurt worse.

"It—it must be washed and some ointment and bandages applied," she said softly.

He drew back involuntarily. "I'd rather leave it for now."

"Absolutely not. You cannot go without care. You'll lose that hand if an infection gets to it."

All he needed was to reenter the time stream, and his hurts would be healed, but he couldn't tell her that. Besides, the very thought of trying to activate the LOC again made him feel weak.

"You're tired," she said, touching his shoulder gently. "You need to rest, sir. But indeed let me do what I can for you first. I know it will hurt dreadfully, but I am a gentle nurse."

She was as good as her word, her touch as tender as her tongue was tart. He bit his tongue bloody to keep from yelling, and when she was done he was sweating freely.

"There," she said, looking as pale as he felt. "I'm sorry. Would you like some brandy? We've used all the laudanum in the house to help poor Peterson—" Her voice caught a little, and she looked very tired and young.

"Thanks, yes," said Noel wearily.

She left the room, and as the door swung closed he thought he heard her crying. In a few minutes, however, she was back with a glass and a brandy bottle. Her eyes were red, but she had washed her face, and seemed her cool, usual self again. She poured him a glass, and while he sipped the fiery liquid, she said, "I've been quite wrong, haven't I? It is you who are the true son, and not the lieutenant."

"What's changed your mind?"

"The signet you wear. It makes everything clear. I can only apologize for the way I've treated you since making your acquaintance this morning. You were so dirty and wild, I thought—But I was mistaken, and I apologize."

He couldn't help glancing at the peg on the back of the door, where Robert had hung his new clothes borrowed from Leon. So a ring and a good wardrobe were all Miss Crewe needed to judge a man's character? He was suddenly thoroughly sorry for her.

She was frowning and looked as though she wanted to question him further.

"I'm tired," he said.

She took the hint at once. "Yes, of course. I'll go and let you sleep."

Noel glanced at Leon in the other bed. "Did you drug him? If he wakes up in the night—"

"You have only to call out, and Robert or I will come," she said, banking the fire. "Good night, sir."

She left, closing the door quietly behind her. Noel frowned for a moment, then threw off the covers and levered himself out of bed. He started shivering again, and his feet were swollen and sore with returning circulation. One-handedly he poured another glass of brandy and tipped it between Leon's lips.

"Drink it all, you devil," he muttered.

Leon murmured and shifted his head away, but Noel finally managed to get the stuff down him. The brandy would not help Leon's fever, but if his duplicate couldn't be tied up, at least let him be drunk. Noel didn't fancy being attacked in his sleep.

He searched his clothing for his pistol and put it under his pillow. Spent from his exertions, he climbed back into bed and tried to get warm again. His chest still hurt and he started coughing again. He dosed himself with brandy, aware that although he'd been packed with all kinds of immunizations and antibacterial agents before he left the Time Institute, pneumonia could still happen. The main thing was to figure out what had gone wrong with the recall sequence. If he could talk to his LOC . . . but he didn't dare activate it. No, he would have to reason it out all by himself.

"Sir! Mr. Kedran!" cried Robert, bursting into the room. "Wake up!"

Startled awake, Noel sat up with a jerk and pulled out his pistol. "What?" He started coughing.

"I'm sorry," said Robert, backing up cautiously and raising his hands. "I didn't mean to startle you, but—but the redcoats are here!"

He pointed at the window as he spoke, and Noel crawled across the bed to peer out. He saw a squadron of mounted soldiers and Sally outside arguing with the sergeant in charge of them.

"Jupiter, won't she be in a taking," said Robert worriedly. "I think she cried herself to sleep, for the major has quite turned against her and now we are to be guarded. It's the most infamous thing."

"Robert," said Noel, coughing, "you had better tell me all you know."

The boy frowned, plainly hesitant. "There isn't time for that. If they come into the house, they may want to search it, and if they find the lieutenant here, we'll all be in jail."

"Aren't you jumping to conclusions?"

"Not when the word is about town that he's been captured by the enemy. A search party went out at dawn, and I heard the major's in a rare pucker. Lieutenant Nardek's indispensable to him."

"I'm sure," said Noel, thinking of Leon's ability to read minds. It would be a handy tool in wartime.

"We're already in enough trouble, and if you're found here, I don't know what will—"

"Okay," said Noel, getting up and reaching one-handedly for his breeches. "We'll clear out."

"Too late for that. We've got to hide you in the cellar. For now, anyway. When it gets dark, I'll try to smuggle you out past them."

The idea of spending the whole day confined in a cellar did not appeal to Noel, but Robert looked so frightened he didn't argue.

Leon was still unconscious since Noel had dosed him with brandy regularly during the night. Dragging Leon from bed, Noel pulled him upright and slipped one shoulder beneath his arm. Leon sagged against him and muttered something unintelligible. He stank of brandy.

Robert opened the door. "Down the back stairs, sir, and hurry!"

"Wait," said Noel, looking around. "It's obvious this room has been used."

"Never mind that, sir. Hannah will see to it." Robert gestured urgently, and Noel maneuvered Leon out.

Getting his duplicate down the stairs was a hazardous, exhausting business. In the pantry, Noel froze as he heard unmistakable sounds of the soldiers coming inside the house.

Robert opened the back door. "Hurry!" he whispered.

They stepped outside into the cold air. Noel's lungs seized up, and he nearly choked himself holding back his coughs. The cellar was dug into the ground, with stone steps leading down to the door. Robert opened this and helped him get Leon inside.

"There's a lantern and tinderbox. I dare not wait for you to light it. I must lock this door and help Hannah."

"Wait—"

But Robert closed the door and shot the bolt home. Plunged into darkness, Noel struck the rough-hewn door once with his good fist. It didn't even rattle. He jerked at the latch, but it didn't budge. He and Leon were effectively locked in.

"Damn!"

Leaving Leon slumped on the floor, Noel leaned against the door to catch his breath. How was he supposed to grope around in pitch darkness to light a lantern he couldn't see?

"Great," he muttered, running his fingers through his hair. "Terrific. Yankee Doodle Dandy."

He started to activate his LOC, but stopped himself. The LOC would provide him with light, yet he didn't think he could endure the pain that would cause. Not yet, anyway.

The place was chilly and damp. It smelled of earth, vegetables, and cider. Noel groped his way forward with caution. Just before Robert had shut the door, he'd seen a table standing in the center of the room with a lantern on it. Probably about five steps away. He counted them off and bumped into the table hard enough to make the lantern rattle.

The Institute had trained him well in all kinds of survival methods. Normally a tinderbox wouldn't be a problem. But Noel was left-handed, and that hand was out of commission. He fumbled and swore and kept trying through failure after failure until he finally managed to strike sparks.

Lantern light spread a yellow glow through the room. He found himself surrounded by stone walls lined with shelves containing numerous crocks of preserves. Nearly empty baskets of apples, sweet potatoes, and turnips stood on the floor. There were plentiful jugs of homemade cider. A few twists of onions hung from the ceiling.

"Some of that cider would be tasty," said Leon's voice from behind him. "Why don't we drink together? Then I can enjoy what you taste."

Tensing, Noel turned slowly around and found Leon standing up. Despite his rumpled nightshirt and bare feet, he showed no signs of his previous illness. His dark gray eyes were absolutely clear and cold.

"That was a fast recovery," said Noel.

Leon raised one brow. "In spite of your nursing efforts? What was all the brandy for? I nearly sickened on it."

"So you were playing possum?"

Leon smiled a taunting, wicked smile. "Your reference has no meaning for me. But it is not important. I—I think it is time to reevaluate matters."

His head twitched violently as he spoke, and he frowned a moment as though trying to bring himself back under control.

"We're hiding in the cellar while soldiers search the house," said Noel. "Your presence here would be an embarrassment."

Leon smirked and started pulling on his clothes that Robert had brought. "I'd still like some cider."

Noel poked around and found a couple of tasting mugs. He filled them with the aromatic liquid, careful to keep his eye on Leon. Then he sat one mug on the table and backed away.

"You act like I'm going to attack you," said Leon, picking it up and drinking deep. He paused. "At least sip some of it. I'm sure it tastes delightful."

Noel took a swallow and frowned as Leon let his eyelids fall half-shut in pleasure. "I thought you were past that type of symbiosis. You haven't been so dependent on me in our last few encounters."

Leon frowned as though he'd forgotten. "Haven't I? It is not important. Did you hurt yourself?"

Noel lifted his bandaged hand briefly. "Yes. Don't you feel it?"

"Why should I?" asked Leon, then looked confused.

"That's right, copy," said Noel harshly. "You're supposed to feel my pain. Symbiosis, remember? You're not acting this part very well."

Leon's face turned red. He twitched and started to fall, then caught himself with a jerk. "I can—I can!"

"Can what? Fool me?" taunted Noel. "I don't think so. For better or worse, I know my duplicate too well. Why don't you leave him alone . . . Qwip?"

Leon stiffened board straight, then his eyes rolled back in his head. A ghostly shape swirled from him to hover in the air, and Leon collapsed in a heap.

"Clever," said Qwip to Noel's mind. "Your intelligence quotient has been underestimated."

Noel stared at the creature hovering before him, trying to absorb what had happened. It had only been a guess. He was shocked to find it was true. "You've been trying to go to my future. Why?"

Qwip shimmered before him, a ghostly outline and nothing more. "This is your theory?"

"No wonder the recall sequence failed," said Noel. "Your kind of matter won't travel along our time stream. You can't enter our dimension, can you?"

Qwip did not reply.

Noel's spirits rose. "Then recall can still work. As long as we're rid of you, we have a chance to repair the—"

"The contact point will remain open," said Qwip.

"Not if Leon and I can recombine. I explained that to you before."

"And I did not fail to understand. We understand even more now."

"Like what?" Noel said impatiently. "What are you getting at?"

"Your words are imprecise—"

"What's your point?"

"When you drifted toward our dimension and began to intrude, we feared destruction. The crossing of dimensions is dangerous."

"Yeah, so?"

"But destruction did not occur. Now we wish to explore. This has presented us with many fascinating opportunities."

Noel stared at the thing. "You want to visit our dimension?"

"I am already within it."

"Not completely," said Noel. "You're not corporeal."

Qwip laughed. "I told you I was showing you a representation of my appearance rather than the truth."

Noel was beginning to get a very bad feeling about this. "Who's we?"

"Is that not obvious? We have learned many things from your duplicate's mind. We will learn more from yours."

As it spoke Qwip separated into three entities, then five, then seven. They surrounded Noel, and suddenly the tiny room seemed filled with them.

He tensed, trying to watch all sides. His heart started beating very fast.

"Merge," commanded Qwip.

They came at him, all at once. Quicker than thought, Noel raised his left hand and shouted, "LOC, activate protection mode!"

Blue light flashed in response, sheathing him. Noel gritted his teeth, and his eyes watered in pain, but he held on, knowing he was safe inside the energy barrier the LOC had created. The entities swarmed about him, but they did not possess him as they had Leon.

Just when he was wondering how much longer this standoff would last, the entities merged back into one vaporous form. It surged toward Leon's body.

"No!" shouted Noel. "LOC, protect Leon too!"

The light surrounding him dimmed, and some of the energy field flowed around Leon.

"Fool!" said Qwip. "You cannot be rid of me that easily."

This time instead of splitting into multiples, Qwip grew, expanding and growing brighter until it almost filled the cellar. The lantern went out. The lack of oxygen made Noel's head spin. He gasped for air, little dots dancing in front of his eyes, and felt his legs weakening beneath him. But he'd rather suffocate than give in.

With a pop, Qwip vanished. Air rushed back into the cellar, and the lantern resumed burning. Noel sank to his knees, gulping in breath after breath until he started coughing. He felt hot and weak.

"LOC, deactivate," he said wearily.

The blue light faded. He sat there a long time on the damp floor, waiting for the agony in his hand to fade.

When he finally felt capable of functioning again, he drew in a ragged breath and poked Leon in the ribs.

"Wake up," he said. "Come on, come on. I need you."

Leon came round slowly, groaning.

"Stop it and snap awake," said Noel. He drew up his knees and rested his throbbing forearm on them. His hand seemed to hurt less when it was elevated.

Leon finally sat up, holding his head in his hands. He looked bleary-eyed, and there was a trickle of blood running from his nostrils.

"You okay?" asked Noel.

Leon shook his head.

"Well, pull yourself together! We've got to get busy."

"Leave me alone," said Leon in a shaking voice. He hunched away.

Noel glared at him. "I need your help."

Leon put his hands over his ears and refused to look at him.

"Poor little you," said Noel harshly. "Possessed by a goblin from another dimension. Stop feeling sorry for yourself."

"It didn't happen to you," said Leon unsteadily.

"Look, in other circumstances I'd let you have the shakes, but I need your help."

"Do it yourself," said Leon with a sniff.

Noel stared at the wall. "I don't think I can," he said hollowly.

That forced Leon to look at him. "What is it?"

"I've got to question the LOC," said Noel, his own courage shrinking as he spoke. "I need it to run an analysis of what happened last night. I need to know if we can still perform a recall."

Leon stared at him in astonishment. "You nearly blew yourself up. The LOC wouldn't take you into the time stream, remember?"

"It wouldn't take Qwip."

Leon shuddered. "I'm glad," he said unconvincingly. "It would have been the end of me."

"And if we stay here, so will Qwip and others like it. Whatever it is!"

"It's loathsome," said Leon. "You think I'm a monster, but it's—"

"I know."

"No, you don't! You can't. It's foul, sickening. It wants—" Leon gasped and drew his hand across his mouth. "I asked you for help, last night. I asked you to help me, and you didn't."

"I couldn't get it out of you," said Noel gently. "I didn't know how."

"Easy to say now!" cried Leon. "You didn't believe me."

"I didn't understand. I do now."

"You wouldn't help me. Why should I help you?"

"Because you know we have to do this. Because you don't want Qwip to come back."

"That's not fair," said Leon.

"I'm sorry. None of this is fair."

"I don't want to die."

"Leon, all I need to do is talk to my LOC."

"Then do it! You don't need me for that."

"Yes, I do."

"It's a trick."

"No."

"You're always full of tricks."

"Now who's lying?"

Leon glared wildly at him, close to hysterics. "I won't! Leave me alone."

Silence fell between them. Noel got to his feet and walked around. "It hurts every time I activate the LOC," he said. "Worse, each time. I don't think I can do it by myself again. I—" He swallowed hard. "I need you to enter my mind and make me forget the pain. You're a telepath. You can do something like that, can't you?"

When he looked around, he found Leon staring at him in astonishment.

"Me?" said Leon. "In contact—direct contact—with your mind? You'd never trust me that far."

"I have to."

Leon laughed, a mirthless, grating sound. "I don't believe you."

Noel just stared at him.

"It can't be done. I can't contact you. I never could."

"You could try."

"It doesn't work, I tell you."

"How do you know?"

"Because I've tried, damn you! I've tried! And there's nothing. I can't even sense you that way."

"But if I let you. If you told me how to let down my guard, and I let you in?"

Leon stared at him. "You're mad."

Noel couldn't meet his gaze. He didn't know whether to be disappointed or relieved. "Then I guess we're finished."

"What do you mean?"

"We're here, forever. Until we're old. Until we die."

Hope lit Leon's eyes. "You mean it?"

Noel nodded.

"We can stay?"

"We have no choice."

"What about automatic recall?"

Noel shrugged. "I don't know if it works anymore. Qwip tampered with the LOC. I've had it effecting self-repairs. I thought it was going to work last night, but Qwip's presence triggered the safety override. I can't access it without your help. I can't—"

He forced himself to look up. "Will . . . will you help me take it off?"

"But you can't remove it!" said Leon, shocked. "Your conditioning."

Noel peeled off the bandages and held out his hand.

Leon whistled softly. "Agony to wear it. Conditioned against taking it off. Are you sure?"

Noel found he was shaking. "I—I can't answer that question."

He sat down abruptly and rested his head on his knees.

"Noel," said Leon in concern. He touched Noel's shoulder hesitantly. He had never touched Noel in kindness before. Before Noel realized it, a lump had filled his throat. He'd never failed like this in his life. Now, everything he'd fought for, believed in, was gone, ruined.

"Noel, don't," said Leon. "What you feel is coming to me. I don't want it. I don't—"

He broke off and knelt before Noel, gripping his shoulders. "All right!" he said roughly. "Damn you, I'll do it. I'll try anyway."

Not believing him, Noel slowly raised his head. His face was wet, but oddly enough it was Leon who looked ashamed.

"It's no good staying here with those Qwip things around," said Leon. "Tell me what to do."

Noel coughed and wiped his face. Leon brought him another mug of cider, and he drank it thirstily.

"Thanks."

"Don't thank me yet," said Leon. "I told you I don't like this. It won't work."

"It's worth a try."

"You're a fool to trust me."

Noel met his eyes, so similar to his own yet so alien. "I know. How do we start?"

"Relax. Make your mind a blank."

Noel shut his eyes and tried to soothe his racing thoughts. It wasn't as easy to relax as he wanted. He was scared.

He coughed, and Leon jumped.

"Dammit, be quiet! How can I concentrate?"

"Sorry," said Noel. It was getting harder all the time to breathe, but this time it wasn't because Qwip was stealing the oxygen.

He shut his eyes and waited. There was nothing for a long while and then he felt a pressure, like a headache that was coming, not here yet, not painful yet, but coming. He frowned, and tried not to resist.

"I hate this," said Leon in his mind.

The words boomed inside Noel's head, much too loud. He winced, and Leon nearly slipped away.

"Be still!" commanded Leon.

"Can you block the pain?"

"How about this?"

Noel waited. "What?"

"Did you feel it?"

"Feel what?"

"I just gripped your injured hand and tried to pull off the LOC. Didn't you feel it?"

"No."

Leon sighed. "Then I guess you'd better get started."

Noel swallowed, but his mouth still felt dry. "LOC," he said slowly, "activate."

CHAPTER 10

The lantern was growing dim by the time there came a furtive scratching at the cellar door. The bolt slid back, and a scared-looking Robert slipped inside.

"I can't stay long," he said breathlessly. "I've come to get the men some cider, and I brought you some food."

He pulled a packet of meat and bread from beneath his coat and laid it on the table.

Noel, sitting on some old feed sacks in the corner, raised his head wearily. "Thanks," he said hoarsely.

"You don't look a bit well," said Robert. "'Pon my soul, you don't. Nor you, Lieutenant."

"Go to hell," said Leon.

Robert stepped back. "Well, I—"

"Don't mind him," said Noel, holding back a cough. "We haven't had a nice day."

Robert sighed. "Nor have we, for that matter. Sally is at her wit's end with this party tonight. I told her she ought to cancel it. It's just too dangerous, but she says she doesn't care. They've planned it too long."

"Planned what?" asked Noel.

Robert glanced at Leon, then cut his eyes back to Noel and shook his head.

Leon laughed. "Oh, speak out, boy. I know about the plot. You might as well tell Noel too."

"I haven't told anyone, sir," said Robert stiffly. "I'm sure I don't know what you mean."

Leon shot Noel a bloodshot look. For a moment his loathing was overlaid with sardonic amusement. "Sally Crewe is holding a ball tonight in honor of Major Burton. While the regiment is here, dancing with all the pretty girls, the local resistance group will meet in the barn with some of Washington's people."

Robert gasped, and one look at his white face told Noel it was true.

"Indeed, no, sir! Sally's a Tory. She's loyal to King George and England."

"Poppycock, to use the local phrase," said Leon with a halfhearted sneer. "If anything is leaked, Sally Crewe has an airtight alibi, right in the arms of her beloved major."

"He's not so beloved today," said Robert bitterly. "Not after he set these guards on us."

"Of course Sally was going to whisper a betrayal in the ear of her major, wasn't she, boy?" said Leon. "Roping up the conspirators in one neat package."

"No!" said Robert in outrage. "She'd never do anything that shabby, that is, if what you said is true, which it isn't."

"Oh, Robert, Robert," sighed Leon. "I tell you we know it all."

Robert stood there, struggling manfully not to let his fear get the better of him.

Noel frowned at his duplicate. "Stop baiting the boy. You're scaring him."

"Why shouldn't he be scared?" retorted Leon. "I'm scared. You're scared. The whole bloody world should be scared."

Robert stared at Leon.

"Don't mind him," said Noel, feeling obliged to soothe the boy. Only he was too tired to care very much. He liked Robert, but right now the boy was an annoyance, and Leon was even more of one. It had been a mistake to ask for Leon's help. If he'd been thinking more clearly at the time, he wouldn't have done it. Now he had a bad taste in his mouth that lingered, and too much regret.

"But, sir," said Robert, "if the major knows all this, then we're—"

"Relax," said Noel. "My twin hasn't told the major anything."

"But Burton knows," said Robert in anguish. "I tried to warn Sally she could be caught, but—"

"Caught at what, betraying the Americans? That's her duty, isn't it?" asked Leon sharply.

His eyes narrowed, and Robert's face went blank.

Noel got up and staggered between them. "Stop it!" he said angrily. "Don't you dare read the boy's thoughts!"

Leon's expression grew surly. "Why shouldn't I? I've been in yours. You whimpered and pleaded until I did that. What's the difference?"

"You know very well what the difference is," said Noel tightly. "Don't do it again."

Leon hissed and turned his face away.

Yes, thought Noel bleakly. *It had been a big mistake. The intimacy was more sour and bitter than ever.*

Robert swayed as Leon's mind released his.

Noel gripped Robert's arm. "Are you all right?"

"Yes." Robert rubbed his forehead in bewilderment. "What happened? I felt all fuzzy and confused suddenly."

"Yes, well, you've been upset over your sister. Try not to worry so much," said Noel, patting his shoulder. "You'd better take your cider now before they wonder where you are."

"Yes, I—I will," said Robert. He picked up the jug and held it pressed against his chest. "Can you help her, sir?"

"How?"

"I don't know. I'm afraid the major has turned against her, if he ever liked her at all. He could implicate her even if she does betray Washington's agent to him."

The trust in the boy's eyes was as disconcerting as his appeal.

"She doesn't trust me," Noel said as gently as he could.

"She doesn't trust anybody," said Robert. "She used to. She used to be on the patriots' side. Back then she just pretended to like the British. But that was before Major Burton was assigned here, and everything changed."

"Triple agent," said Leon scornfully.

Robert turned red.

"Ignore him," said Noel.

"But he's the major's adjutant," whispered Robert.

"Not anymore. Run along."

"But what are we to do?"

"I'll think of something. Go on."

Leon stood up. "And don't lock the door again."

Robert looked more upset. "But Sally said it was safer for you."

"Don't," said Leon.

Robert's gaze dropped from his. "All right." He started out, then glanced back at Noel. "Please help her, sir. If you can."

"I'll try."

Robert nodded and hurried away. Noel closed the door.

"Help her?" said Leon with scorn. "How? You can't even help yourself."

Noel glared at him. "I told you not to tamper with the boy's mind."

Leon shrugged. "Why should we be locked in here like rats? I'm tired of it."

"This is as good a place to wait for the LOC to effect self-repair as any."

"Hours, it said." Leon laughed scornfully. "You're a fool to keep hoping."

He'd been sulking ever since they broke mental contact. It was as though he'd finally accepted the fact that Noel would never give up on trying to take him back.

"Do you want some food?" asked Noel.

"Why? So you can tell me how good it tastes?" Leon flung himself around and picked up his coat. "I'm getting out of here."

"Don't be stupid," said Noel. "You know Qwip is out there somewhere. It could have possessed one of the soldiers. Maybe Sally or one of her servants. It would rather have you or me, though. Why give it the opportunity until we're ready?"

"You mean until you're ready," Leon said with a sneer. "The LOC can do repairs all day long, and you still aren't going to get back. It won't work. It can never work. You say we have to be recombined, well, weren't we? The last time? We went through the time stream together, didn't we, and it ripped us apart again. That's because we're *not* supposed to be together. Your theory is wrong. It always was. I'm not a part of you. I'm a copy of you. You're not less than whole without me. You couldn't function if that were true. I'm just a reflection, that's all. Why can't you accept that?"

"Maybe I can," said Noel slowly. "But I still know the time anomaly happened because we were in different centuries. We have to be together. If not recombined, then at the same point in history."

"And if we stay here, we have Qwip to deal with," said Leon bitterly. He paced back and forth like a caged animal. "Even if your LOC can reestablish contact with the time portal, there's no guarantee of success. You're crazy if you try again."

"You know I will."

"Not with me."

"Leon, we can argue till sundown and it won't change anything. I'm entering the time stream as soon as the LOC is ready. And I'll make you go with me."

"Hah!"

"Don't you want to stop Qwip?"

Leon stopped with his hand on the door. His shoulders were rigid. "I," he said softly, "am going to let Qwip have what he wants."

"Leon, no!"

"Why not?" asked Leon, glancing at him. "Don't forget I was in your thoughts. I know all about your encounter with the thing between dimensions. Qwip told you he wanted us recombined. Qwip told you he was on your side. But it's a lie. He proved that today."

"Exactly. We can't trust him. And there's no telling what will happen if—"

"Get this straight," broke in Leon. "I don't care what happens."

Noel frowned. "But you must. Leon—"

Shaking his head, Leon opened the cellar door.

Noel threw himself across the room and slammed it shut. Breathless from even that minor exertion, he choked back a cough and gripped Leon by the arm. "Don't be a fool. You—"

Leon pushed him roughly away. "Get off me."

He and Noel coughed in unison.

"See?" said Leon furiously. "You're absorbing me again, making me feel what you feel. I can't stay with you. I won't suffer with you. I have to get away."

"Leon—"

"No!"

And Leon wrenched open the door and ran up the steps into the daylight.

Cursing, Noel went out after him, but Leon was too quick. By the time Noel emerged from the stairwell into the afternoon sunlight, Leon was out of sight. Hearing voices, Noel ducked down into the cellar again. He waited, tensed by the door, but there came no sounds of commotion or of discovery.

Slowly he let out his breath, relieved that Leon hadn't gone to the soldiers.

During their time of contact, Noel hadn't been able to read Leon's thoughts, but he sensed that Leon was up to something with that devious brain of his. Leon already knew about the trap laid for the patriots who would be meeting in secret tonight. Chances were that he intended to work that to his own advantage.

As for Qwip, Noel shook his head. Leon's memory was very short-term, but Noel's wasn't. He knew Qwip had lied and manipulated, and would do so again. He wanted to consult his LOC for more theories on how to close the door on Qwip forever, but even with Leon's help, activating the LOC had been exhausting. He'd focused on finding out how long it would take the LOC to repair itself, and then he'd cut it off.

Now, however, he stared at his bandaged hand, wondering if he had found his courage again. No, if he activated the LOC, it would have to divert power and attention away from its self-repairs. The more he left it alone, the sooner it would be ready to send him home.

"Thinking about me?" said an unearthly voice in his mind. "I am honored."

For a crazy moment he thought the LOC was speaking to him. Then Qwip's ghostly form descended from the ceiling and hovered between Noel and the door.

He tensed, more frightened of the thing than he wanted to admit. His heartbeat speeded up, and he was conscious of his lungs struggling against the fluid that was accumulating inside them. He tried not to cough and wished he hadn't been so worried about Qwip going after Leon again. It looked like he was the target this time.

"You do not protect yourself now," said Qwip. "Interesting. You are conserving the energy of your device."

"Maybe," said Noel, keeping his eyes on the creature that formed and re-formed before him. Watching Qwip was almost hypnotic. He took care not to stare too closely.

"We are learning about the variety of your kind," said Qwip. "This fascinates us."

"I think you should go back to where you belong."

"The original unit is stronger and more intelligent than the copy. This is logical to us."

"Flattery will get you nowhere."

"Leon was unsatisfactory. His pattern is that he lets fear consume him, then he takes no action."

Noel frowned. That wasn't exactly true, but he saw no need to correct Qwip's assessment.

"You utilize your emotions. We find this variation . . . interesting. The other units at these coordinates are primitive. They have no understanding of technology or of time."

"Yeah, well, your zoological studies should end right there," said Noel. "I can promise you that no one in this time is going to be advanced." He wasn't about to mention Thomas Jefferson or Benjamin Franklin, and hoped Qwip wasn't scanning his mind right now.

"We wish to visit your time."

Alarmed, Noel backed up a step. "You can't! You tried that already. You can't enter our time stream."

"You are incorrect. It was the copy who could not return. We believe the original will have no difficulties."

Noel took another step back. His heart was hammering now. He held up his bandaged hand. "You're not going to take possession of me. The LOC won't let you."

As he spoke he waited for Qwip to split into multiples, but this time none appeared. There was only Qwip swirling before him. And Qwip began to alter, right before his eyes, until the face and form of Sally Crewe stood before him. She was ghostly white, translucent in places, but otherwise a very good replica.

She smiled, and it was Sally's smile—rare and alluring. "This appeals to you," whispered Sally's voice in his mind. "This appeals to you most strongly."

Qwip was wrong; it was Leon who had fallen for Sally. Noel was aware of her attraction, but he didn't like her personality. He said nothing and wondered why Qwip didn't read his mind.

"You've looked at me," she whispered. "You are jealous of your commander. Each time he kisses my hand you burn with the desire to be in his place. Now is your chance. Let me come to you. Let me be a part of you. This is an intimacy suited for you. How many women have you kissed, only to wonder what the feelings really are? How many have you reached for with your mind, only to have them crumble? I am for you. Let me come into your thoughts. Let me be a part of you."

That seductive whisper in his mind was enticing. But it was speaking to the wrong man. Noel was surprised at first, then amazed at Qwip's mistake. How had Qwip confused him with Leon? He relaxed, aware that this tactic wasn't going to work.

Qwip struck with a speed faster than thought. The ghostly vision of Sally enveloped Noel, and he was drowning in it, blinded by a pale mist, the clammy sensation of something alien on his skin, sinking in.

"LOC!" he shouted. "Activate protection—"

His LOC responded with one flash of blue light, then was suddenly extinguished. With it went Noel's hope. He had been tricked, and the amusement pouring into him confirmed it.

He struggled, but Qwip had him, was being absorbed into him. If he screamed, there was no sound.

"Do not fight me," said the alien thoughts in his mind. "Do not fight. It makes assimilation more unpleasant for you. Think of Sally."

Noel staggered back until he crashed into the table. The lantern rolled off and crashed to the floor. Little flames spurted up, racing toward the storage baskets.

"I don't want Sally, damn you!" shouted Noel. "Get out!"

"If you struggle, you make it harder. Enjoy yourself. I am a part of you now."

"Never!"

Choked by the smoke rapidly filling the cellar, Noel pushed himself away from the table and staggered to the wall. He bumped into the shelves, and crocks went crashing to the floor. Some of them shattered, and he tripped over the pieces. He was blind, unable to see anything but Qwip's whiteness. His whole body convulsed, trying to reject this thing that had entered him. His hands flailed out, and dragged the shelves down. A crock hit his shoulder, another his head. The blow stunned him. He dropped to his knees. There was heat, and the crackling of flames. He reached out blindly and felt the fire catch his sleeve. Pain seared up his arm. He cried out, rolling to escape it, and still Qwip did not release him.

"LOC!" he cried. "LOC, activate!"

"LOC has malfunctioned," said Qwip in his mind. It slithered through him, coiled around his thoughts, drove him mad. "LOC is busy. LOC will take us to your future . . . later."

"No!" shouted Noel.

Better to die than to be possessed. He flung himself toward the fire, but his body was jerking to other commands. Brought to his feet, he found himself turned around.

He could see now, although dimly, through the smoke. It choked him, making him cough. His eyes watered from the stuff.

Must start the fire, he thought hazily, then realized his thoughts were wandering. He wasn't in England; he was in Pennsylvania. This was a different fire. This was a different time and a different danger.

The fire blazed across the rear of the cellar. Baskets charred and popped. A keg of cider exploded in the heat.

Die, he thought. *If I die, Qwip dies.*

"No," said Qwip and jerked him in the other direction toward the door. "You will live, and you will serve me!"

"Never!" shouted Noel. He slammed his injured hand against the rough oak panels of the door, and the resulting agony broke some of Qwip's control. With all the strength he possessed, Noel flung himself back into the fire.

CHAPTER 11

Reality shift:

COMMUNICATION . . . *Qwip activation ill advised. Recommendation to terminate activity.*

COMMUNICATION . . . *Disagreement. Qwip successfully tracking intruders. Termination of intruders highly advisable.*

COMMUNICATION . . . *Examination of intruder mind unsatisfactory. Multiple mind levels create imprecise analysis. Qwip insufficiently sophisticated for this task.*

COMMUNICATION . . . *Disagreement. Qwip successfully tracking intruders.*

COMMUNICATION . . . *Disagreement. Qwip not tracking intruders for termination. Qwip tracking intruders for alternate purpose. Qwip reaching range limits. Danger is foreseen.*

COMMUNICATION . . . *Qwip will not deviate from designed course activity.*

COMMUNICATION . . . *Correction. Qwip has deviated.*

∞ ∞ ∞

COMMUNICATION . . . *Qwip adaptable to circumstances. Intruders must be terminated. At source, if necessary.*

COMMUNICATION . . . *Postulation. If Qwip remains within control range but can terminate intruders at source, then activity is satisfactory.*

COMMUNICATION . . . *Concurrence requested.*

COMMUNICATION . . . *Concurrence offered.*

INSTRUCTIONS . . . *Increase control range of Qwip activity.*

CHAPTER 12

Leon staggered past the barn and its pens of livestock down a slight slope to a stream. He sat on a stone and stared blankly at the trees beyond. He was breathing hard. Now and then his body twitched in small spasms beyond his control. He tried to close his mind, tried to cut off the empathic link between him and Noel, but it didn't work. He knew what was happening.

Noel's panic reached him like a knife thrust across space. He gasped, pressing his fists to his chest, then the emotion faded. In its place came a leap of iron-hard determination.

Aghast, Leon jumped to his feet. "No, Noel!" he whispered. "Let it take you. Let it—*no*!"

He spun around, horrified at Noel's plan. Suicide over possession? It wasn't possible. Noel would never dare. He wouldn't—

There came the smell of smoke, harsher and more acrid than simple woodsmoke. He could smell burning cloth, burning hair, burning flesh. Agony reached him and drove him to his knees.

He wept, pounding his fists on the ground, then staggered up, intending to run back and stop him.

The contact vanished.

So suddenly did it go, Leon stumbled and nearly fell. He propped himself against a tree, gasping for breath. Sweat and tears streaked his face.

He felt free, isolated. All contact with Noel had been severed.

It should have been a relief to be released from that bondage. His chest no longer felt constricted. He no longer felt mildly feverish. His hand no longer ached. Noel's pains had faded from him. Noel's emotions no longer beat at him. Noel was simply . . . gone.

"Possessed," whispered Leon. "You're possessed, you fool. You are not dead! You cannot be dead!"

He told himself it was stupid to worry. He'd thought Noel dead several times before, and always he had been wrong. Once before Noel had been possessed by a thing of black magic, and Leon had not been released like this.

He told himself he did not care.

But in his heart he knew better.

His thoughts turned back to that last hour in the cellar with Noel. Qwip had not left as Noel believed. Qwip had communicated with Leon, their exchange undetected by Noel. Stupid Noel, who would never know the advantages of telepathy. It had been a simple deal, an open trade. Noel should have listened when Leon said he would do anything Qwip wanted. After all, Leon's own safety was offered in exchange for leaving Noel alone where Qwip could get at him. He had told Qwip how to trick Noel too.

What was the harm? It would do Noel good to have a little taste of possession by that horrifying, creeping essence. When Leon had asked for his help against Qwip, Noel hadn't paid attention. When Leon had begged, Noel had ignored him. Later, when Qwip was out of him and gone, Noel hadn't been sympathetic to Leon at all. Noel was always focused on himself. As far as Noel was concerned, Leon's welfare didn't matter. But now Noel was gone and Leon was free.

Inexplicably he struck the tree with his fist and began to cry. It wasn't in him to choose death over slavery. Why was Noel different? Why did he always have these stupid principles? Why did he have to be heroic? It wasn't fair.

If Noel was gone, what would happen to him?

They'd been closely entwined at the very first, so close Leon almost could not breathe without Noel. Then as they had traveled from time to time, that clinging symbiosis had faded. Leon had become his own entity, strong enough in his own right to cease feeling what Noel felt. He had tried to kill Noel then, and failed because of Noel's trickery. But now, it was almost as though they had gone back to the beginning.

Time loop, said his thoughts.

But Leon couldn't believe he was dependent on Noel again. He'd existed three months without Noel. He'd been able to eat and enjoy food. He'd been real. He'd been alive.

Until Noel came. Then they had begun to merge again. And now . . . if Noel was a dead man, then so would Leon die.

Shouts roused him from his self-pity. He looked around in alarm and was tempted to run. But past experience had taught him that he was more vulnerable away from people. Reluctantly he returned to the barn, and concealed himself inside it, watching through a crack between the boards as the Crewe servants and the soldiers formed a bucket brigade to put out the fire in the root cellar.

They barely prevented it from spreading to the main house. But at last the flames were beaten, and only smoke hung in the air. The dead winter grass had been burned away almost to the back steps of the house. Sally was weeping, and Robert had his arm around her. The sergeant went down the steps himself and came back quickly, shaking his head.

Leon felt his entrails twist and he found himself gnawing like a wild creature on one of the boards. Was Noel dead? *Was he?* Would they next drag up the charred corpse?

The people talked and shook their heads and presently dispersed. There was no corpse. Therefore, somehow Noel had escaped. He was not dead.

Leon slowly sank back in the straw, embittered with himself rather than relieved. What good was a hatred if he flung it away the moment he thought Noel was dead? What kind of fool was he to feel guilt over a betrayal that had come to nothing? He had even wept for Noel, idiot that he was. That infuriated him more than anything else. It must have been the contact with Noel's mind that had contaminated him, weakened him. He spat, feeling hollow with disgust. Never again would he expend the slightest amount of pity for Noel. Never again would he let himself care, or feel sorry. If Noel thought he was a monster, now let Noel see what he could do.

For Leon knew something that neither the British nor Sally Crewe knew. It wasn't Washington's messenger who would be coming tonight to meet secretly under the very noses of the British. It was Washington himself. And Leon planned to change history so thoroughly the whole world would stagger from it. Noel would never again be able to make a last-minute save. And Qwip could go on as many rampages as it liked.

Accordingly, Leon kept himself concealed through the rest of the afternoon. He amused himself by prowling through the minds of the soldiers, eavesdropping on their thoughts and conversations. He knew he was still missing, believed captured. For now, it suited his purposes to stay out of sight. If he turned up, Burton would expect a report. Leon loathed reports. Besides, he was no longer certain he meant to stay an army officer. His little experiment in playing by the rules now bored him. He wanted to destroy. He wanted to make mayhem. He wanted to loot and hurt.

Night came at last, and a full white moon rose over the land. It was a traveling moon, bright and clear. The house blazed with light, musicians practiced their tunes, and carriages began to arrive. Some came for the lavish dinner; others arrived later for the dancing. People called out merry greetings. There was much laughter and revelry. Sentries shivered at their posts, but there was a housemaid to take them a measure of warm grog. Coachmen and grooms lounged in the warmth of the barn, dicing by lantern light.

Leon skulked through the shadows, keeping himself on the fringes of activity, unnoticed in the general confusion. Since the barn was occupied, where was the meeting to be held? He had missed something, and it annoyed him.

He began to wish he had reported to Burton. Then he might be standing inside the house among the guests. He could see Sally, radiant in a silk ball gown, the slender curve of her throat pure and white, the fullness of her breasts white against her dress, her eyes alight with daring. Why couldn't it be him her eyes shone for? But she never saw him. Burton was the only man she cared for, that lanky piece of arrogance, who thought himself better than anyone because of his name and his aristocratic lineage. The marriage fantasies clouding Sally's brain would come to nothing. Burton was engaged to his cousin, a young lady he never mentioned. He found Sally an amusing armful and a useful dupe, nothing more.

Eager for a glimpse of her, Leon pressed himself against a window of the house and peered inside at the guests. He had no lineage. Even his name was a corruption of Noel's, but he would never lie to Sally, never belittle her, never use her. Only he had no chance of winning her heart, and he knew it the way a cripple knows he will never walk.

But after tonight, she would know he existed. She would look at him with admiration instead of indifference. She would never again ignore him. No one could.

He heard something, sensed it from far away. His head turned, and he left the window, merging more deeply into the inky gloom of the garden shrubbery. The shadows were coming, riding in smoke silent, leaving their horses far away to finish the approach on foot, coming from different directions, caution uppermost in their minds.

Leon sniffed the air, aware that the dogs tonight had been chained in the stable. There was nothing to give the alarm. Oh, his Sally was a cool one. He bided his time, singling out a sentry. When the man was alone and his back was turned, Leon struck him down and dragged him into the bushes. He took the man's pistol and ran. He slipped past the kitchen, past the charred root cellar, past the well, past the barn, past the chicken house, past the servants' quarters, and out to the empty granary with its round walls and lack of windows. There he blended into the shadows and waited, as silent as the night, for his quarry to come.

Inside the house, Noel sat wedged inside a linen storage cupboard. His cramped legs had long since gone to sleep on him. He had stuffed the corner of a sheet in his mouth to muffle his coughing, and the linen cloth tasted awful. His clothing was scorched, his eyebrows had been singed, and he was suffering from several painful burns, but it had been worth it to drive Qwip out. Since his escape from the root cellar, he had seen Qwip twice, hovering watchfully just at the corners of his vision. But Qwip had not approached him again. He supposed the creature was trying to reevaluate its next move. For all its lying and changes of direction, Qwip did not appear to think quickly when confronted with the unexpected. Qwip might want to go with him to the future, but it did not want to die in the effort. As long as he had that bluff on the creature, Noel suspected it would leave him alone.

As for Leon, he knew his duplicate was lurking about, up to some devilment. Leon was not likely to stray far when he had the chance to cause trouble.

So Noel had hidden himself, overhearing the Crewes' puzzlement as to what had become of him and Leon. Preparations for the ball had gone on all day. People had tramped up and down the stairs, but no one had come here for linens. Noel might be cramped in his hiding place, but the rest had done him good. He felt somewhat better, although he was still feverish and achy.

When the musicians struck up a lively reel, and the babble of guests commenced downstairs, Noel emerged cautiously. Taking off his shoes, he crept along the passageway in his stockinged feet and knocked upon a door.

No one replied. He opened it and let himself inside the still room.

Here was where Sally kept her herbal mixtures and household cures as well as stores of candles, oil, beeswax, scouring pumice, string, pickling spice, and salt. Noel poked swiftly through the herbs and elixirs, sniffing and grimacing. Most of it looked like nasty stuff indeed. He found an empty bottle of laudanum, and put it down hastily. He didn't need any opium derivatives. Finally, however, he found a few suitable herbs and mixed them with honey to make himself a sort of cough syrup. It didn't taste too bad, and it soothed his throat.

Going out into the passageway, he went exploring until he came to the largest bedroom. No doubt it had belonged to Sally's late father. The bed had been stripped and the mattress rolled up for storage. There was a closed, musty smell in the room. Personal belongings of the late master had been cleared away. But inside the clothes press, Noel found some clothing that he exchanged for his burned and torn garments. The breeches were too short; the coat was too large around. But at least he no longer smelled quite as smoky. Noel peered at himself in the mirror and gave his face a spit bath to clear the smudges away. He combed his dark hair and parted it on the other side.

Then he went downstairs the back way, avoiding the busy servants, and slipped out into the darkness. Picking up a wooden pail and a dipper, he made his way busily along, keeping his face always in the shadows.

"Water? No thanks," laughed a sentry, when approached. "Not after this good grog, I ask you."

Noel glanced around; no one else was near or paying attention. He slung the empty pail against the sentry's head, knocking off his hat and sending him sprawling. The man lay still, quite unconscious.

"You should have had a drink," murmured Noel.

Dragging him out of sight, Noel stripped him quickly to his underwear. He gagged the soldier with his own handkerchief and put on the uniform, taking care to remove the rank insignia. Then he touched his fingertip to the trickle of blood running down the unconscious sentry's face and smeared it on his shirt.

He slipped past the pond and around it to the lane, keeping out of sight. From this angle the house looked handsome, shining with light and merry with welcome. The guests were still arriving, the men in powdered wigs, the women decked out in silken finery. Noel thought of his march with Washington's wounded troops, thought of the cold and misery of that night, thought of the turnip he'd been given to eat. He found himself amazed that the army had persevered at all in the face of such civilian indifference to the cause of freedom.

But it was time for his own performance. He started up the lane. He did not get very close to the house before a sentry with a bayonet confronted him.

"Stand and identify yourself!" he barked.

Noel's fever had risen from his exertions. He did not have to pretend fatigue. Bending over with a bout of coughing, he managed to choke out, "Nardek."

"What?" gasped the soldier. "Lieutenant Nardek? Sir! We feared you'd been captured by the Americans."

Still coughing, Noel nodded.

"A lantern here! Sharp! And some of that grog."

Noel didn't want any rum, but the men pressed around, one throwing a cloak over his shoulders, another putting a cup in his hand. They were full of eager questions.

Noel fended them off, saying, "Must report to the major."

"Yes, sir! Owens, run ahead and find the sergeant."

The private ran to obey.

"Just you lean on Corporal Masters," said the sentry. "God bless your safe return, sir."

Nodding and accepting their congratulations, Noel walked up to the house with the support of the corporal. He was met at the steps by a sergeant, who took a scowling look at him before rapping out orders for word to be passed to Lieutenant Wilcox.

"You look fair done in, sir," said the sergeant. "All right, Corporal. I've got him in hand now. Carry on."

"Yes, sir!"

With a salute, the corporal scurried back to his post.

"Let's get you inside to a fire. You're fair shaking and no wonder, sir."

The entry to the house had been cleared, but the officers attending the ball had abandoned their partners to crowd in, and the civilians craned their necks beyond. As he made his way through the crowd, Noel saw Sally Crewe standing on the stairs, where she'd been receiving her guests.

She wore a satin dress as blue as her eyes. It was cut low off her shoulders, and her strand of pearls was as lustrous as her fair skin. She wore her golden hair swept up to display her lovely neck. Her face had gone completely white.

Their eyes met, his steady and hers fearful. Then he noticed the sandy-haired man standing next to her in dress regimentals. Thin, tall, rawboned, Major Burton had a jutting nose and piercing brown eyes beneath a set of thick eyebrows. He stared at Noel while one of his adjutants hastened to his side and whispered in his ear.

The major nodded and said something to Sally, who stood frozen.

"What is it?" asked a woman. "What's happened? I do not understand."

"Just this moment escaped," murmured someone else.

They all stared at Noel, who could feel the sweat popping out on his brow. He held himself still, trying not to let his nerves get away from him. When the major finally succeeded in pushing his way through the crowd, Noel drew himself erect, away from the supporting hand of the sergeant, and saluted.

"Lieutenant Nardek reporting, sir! I—"

The room was suddenly very hot. All their faces rushed at him and he forgot what he'd been about to say.

There was a commotion, and then Noel came to, finding himself sitting in a chair in the parlor, an adjutant holding smelling salts under his nose, and the major pacing slowly around the room with a deep frown on his face.

The smelling salts were horrible. Noel grimaced and pushed them away.

"He's coming round, sir."

"Eh?" Burton came over at once.

"Poor devil," said the adjutant. "He's had a rotten time of things, from the look of him. Tortured, there's no doubt. And see how they've insulted him, stripping off his rank."

"Yes," said Burton slowly. "Not Washington's usual style, to treat prisoners in such a fashion. Or did the Indians get hold of you?"

Noel shook his head and tried to stand up.

"No, no, my dear Nardek," said Burton, pressing his shoulder. "Keep your chair. You need a doctor."

"Must report," said Noel.

"Yes, and so you shall. I am anxious to hear what you discovered. But slowly, my good fellow. Don't distress yourself. You need rest and attention first."

Noel gripped at his sleeve. "Can't wait."

He cast Burton a look, then started coughing.

"Ah, Wilcox," drawled Burton, "run and fetch the lieutenant a glass of water. There's a good chap."

"Yes, sir."

Wilcox hurried out, shutting the door firmly on the curious onlookers still gathered outside. Noel heard him urging people to return to their dancing. In a moment the music resumed.

"You ran more risk than I expected," said Burton. "I hope for your sake it was worth it. You'll want a promotion for this bravery, I'll warrant. Then I shan't have you as an adjutant. You know how much I value your services."

With difficulty Noel held his expression neutral. Inside he felt disgust for his duplicate. Leon must have wormed and fawned over this guy.

"Well, then, what have you learned?" asked Burton. "Is it true that Washington's troops are well trained?"

Noel nodded.

"Blast that Prussian turncoat! He's been drilling them all winter, no doubt."

"Looks that way," said Noel.

"And communications from the French? Has Washington received any?"

Noel shook his head. "I think that has fallen through."

Burton chuckled and rubbed his hands. "Not the way the wind's been blowing lately, is it? I'll warrant the patriots are crushed over that disappointment. We all know they cannot continue without French support."

Noel said nothing, waiting for his next cue. If his memory was correct, the French would ally themselves officially with America in the next month or two. Burton was going to be a very surprised officer.

The major clasped his hands at his back and mused aloud, "So no help from the French, eh? They've enough unrest in their own country, from what I hear. I'm sure the diplomats muddled it. These colonials are fools if they think they have enough sophistication to negotiate treaties with foreign heads of state." He swung around eagerly. "And the spring campaign? Did you discover anything there? Did you see any maps? Where will he move first?"

Noel shook his head, and the eagerness in Burton's face dimmed to a scowl.

"Oh, dash and blast, man! The very thing most vital. How am I to outthink this upstart if I don't have the necessary information?"

"They were more concerned with a meeting of some kind," said Noel.

"Yes, I know all about that," said Burton impatiently. "Another futile attempt to stir up resistance among the populace, as though any of these fat farmers cared a tuppence for the trouble the firebrands in Boston wish to cause."

"But—"

"Oh, it's as good as settled. The meeting is to be here, tonight. Sally's already told me. I expect to round up and jail a few of the troublemakers, then the others will fall back into line and we'll have no more unrest for a while."

Noel looked at him blankly. "Why would they come here, sir?"

"Dash it, to thumb their noses at us. That's the American mind for you, always running a dare or a bluff with nothing to back it up. They think we're too stupid to suspect them of risking a meeting here while the place is swarming with my men. But of course we know all about it."

"Do we?" said Noel.

"Hmm? What do you mean, Nardek? What're you getting at?"

Noel shook his head. "I heard nothing about it being here."

"Blast your eyes," cried Burton in amazement. "You're the one who put me on to Sally's treachery in the first place."

Noel could have kicked Leon. So much for Leon's liking the girl. His duplicate was more twisted than he'd suspected. "Well, it's what I had pieced together. But either I had it wrong or they changed the meeting place. It won't be here."

"Where, then?"

Wilcox returned at that moment with a glass in his hand. Burton waved at him impatiently to shut the door.

Noel reached for the glass of water, but Burton all but knocked it from his hand.

"Drink that later. Where, man? If you know at all, speak up!"

"Ollenby's," said Noel, and went into a fit of coughing.

Burton and Wilcox stared at each other.

"Dispatch the men," said Burton.

"Right away, sir."

"Move!"

"Yes, sir."

Wilcox scuttled out, and Burton paced the room, fuming.

"I won't be made a fool of by these colonials. By God, I won't! As for Sally—"

Noel looked up. "She's not involved."

"Not involved?" repeated Burton, boggling at him. "Good God, I made the little minx a double agent. How couldn't she be involved?"

Before Noel could invent a response, the door opened and Sally came in. She was still very pale, and her eyes went from him to Burton and back to him.

"Sir," she said unsteadily, "I have just this moment received confirmation from my servant. The traitors are meeting in the—"

"By God, Sally, enough," snapped Burton while Noel tried unsuccessfully to catch her eye. "I know the truth of tonight's business. You won't catch me out again."

"But I tell you they're—"

"No, they are not here," he said firmly. "Lieutenant Nardek has told me the truth of the conspiracy and I've already dispatched my men."

Her mouth opened. She looked flabbergasted and stared at Noel as though she could not believe her eyes. "Lieutenant, what does this mean?"

"Don't badger the man," said Burton. "Can't you see how badly he's been handled? By God, until now I took them for halfway civilized men, but I can see they've no more notion of how to receive a prisoner properly than they know how to fight."

She was still staring at Noel. He saw recognition dawn in her eyes and waited for her to betray him, but she did not. Pressing her fan to her lips, she sat down on the nearest chair. "I do not understand," she said at last.

"Qualms, my dear?" asked Burton, rather unpleasantly. "It's no good turning squeamish. You've been playing against me, but it's caught up with you."

"No, indeed I haven't, Thomas!" she cried out. "I swear I—"

"Please, let's not have a womanish scene," he said with impatience. "I always liked your spirit, my dear. Don't lose it now."

"I tell you I am not mistaken. I don't care what you've been told. The conspirators have come here and are at the granary this instant. If you do not move quickly, you will lose them all."

He snorted and looked away from her. Noel scowled at her, wishing she would shut up.

She rose to her feet and walked toward Burton. "How can I convince you? Have I lost your trust so completely just because of a visitor to my house? I—"

"Visitor?" he said, swinging around. "My God, woman, a known courier for—"

"I gave you his secret communiqué," she said desperately and caught at Burton's sleeve.

He shook her off. "And that is probably false too, for all I know."

"I would not lie to you, Thomas. I would not betray you."

"Wouldn't you? Are you not an American? Was your father not one of Franklin's friends?"

"I am loyal to the crown." She was weeping now, tears streaking her lovely face. "Please, Thomas, don't shout at me like this. Not in front of—"

"Why should we hide it from Nardek? He's carried messages between us often enough to know how the land lies."

She pressed her hands to her cheeks. "How cold you are. How hard."

"You are a deceiving strumpet, flirting with me while your friends commit treason. Well, you're not free of that taint, my dear. You'll go before a judge with the rest of them."

"But I've been working for you!" she said.

"Then you are doubly contemptible," he retorted. "Tell me this, Sally. Having betrayed your own friends as well as your father's, do you expect me to believe you would not betray me also?"

"Oh!" she cried. "You make monstrous accusations. It is you who have deceived me, sir, from the very beginning."

"I made you no promises, Sally."

She looked up, her eyes dark with tears, and said nothing.

"Go back to your guests, my dear," he continued in an airy voice. "I'll join you presently when Nardek is settled here. After all, this ball is in my honor, and I shan't be found lacking in my good manners to you and your company."

"No," she whispered.

"Ah, yes. Your mind is still quick for a woman's, isn't it? When the ball is over, I shall arrest you. Until then, try to enjoy yourself."

She stood there, trying without success to brush away her tears. "I tell you I have been true. What I did would be despicable to some. I never cared, thinking I did it for you. But if you think me contemptible, then I—" Her voice broke and she had to swallow before she could carry on.

"Sir—" said Noel in a low voice, unable to see her so upset.

Burton shook his head. "No, my boy. I believe you rather than her. There is no secret meeting here. That we are sure of."

Just as he finished speaking, a shot rang out. In the ballroom women screamed, and the music died on the wail of a wrong note. Noel jumped to his feet and hurried to the window.

"It came from outside," said Burton, already striding toward the door. "Sergeant!"

He flung open the door and issued a stream of orders. Soldiers were already running through the darkness behind the house. A series of gunshots rang out, and there were more screams from the guests. A mad scramble took place as people rushed for safety.

"My God!" said Sally. "What is it?"

Noel gripped her wrist. "Your precious meeting has gone wrong, I think."

"But you said—"

He shot her a look of exasperation. "Unlike you, I was lying through my teeth. Come on!"

CHAPTER 13

In the general uproar of hysterical guests and officers shouting for horses and weapons, no one noticed Noel leading Sally to the back of the house. At the rear door, a guard challenged Noel but backed off when Noel said, "She's a prisoner, by Major Burton's orders."

He plucked a cloak off a peg and threw it around Sally's shoulders, then rushed her outside. She was still weeping and seemed not to care where he took her.

As soon as they gained the safety of darkness, he gripped her by the arms and shook her. "Get hold of yourself," he said urgently. "There's no time to cry. I know you've got courage. Show it now!"

She sniffed but her voice was steadier as she asked, "What do you intend for me?"

"To save you, if I can."

"How—"

"Don't worry about that now. I've got to see what Leon's done."

He strode on, keeping a tight grasp on her wrist, and she stumbled along beside him. She wasn't dressed for the cold air, and her dancing slippers were too thin for the rough ground, but she made no complaint.

Past the kitchen, all was a milling confusion of soldiers armed with muskets. Officers were shouting, trying to form them into orderly search parties. Noel looked at the other buildings and saw a furtive shadow flit by.

"Keep your head down," he said and ran.

She kept pace with him until a volley of shots rang out. Noel slung her into the bushes. "Stay there!" he commanded and ducked low around the corner of the barn. The British were returning fire now, ragged and still out of order. Noel pressed his shoulders to the wall and tried to catch his breath. Inside he could hear frightened horses and cattle moving around. Soldiers were coming up on his left. He ducked to the right and dashed behind a stack of fodder. The moonlight was still bright, and he watched until he saw movement. Shots rang out again, and he ran as hard as he could toward the granary.

He made it, but just barely, flinging himself flat to the ground beneath a barrage of musket fire. A huddle of the conspirators were grimly keeping the British from surrounding the granary, buying time for those at the rear who were mounting up.

Noel started to get closer, then ducked as two men dragged a struggling figure toward the riders. "Got him, General!" said one in a triumphant whisper. "Damned sneaking spy, daring to take a potshot at you!"

"General, this way!" whispered someone else. "There's no time."

"Aye, go, sir. We'll slit this one's gullet—"

"No," said Washington's firm deep voice. "Is he in uniform?"

"Aye, a damned redcoat."

"Let him go," said Washington. "We need no prisoners tonight."

"But, sir!"

"Come, sir, please!"

A yell came from the soldiers, and Washington and his entourage galloped away, splitting into two groups and forcing the British pursuers to divide themselves in order to follow.

"It's all or nothing, lads," said one of the few remaining patriots. They opened fire again, and Noel had to duck low.

"Orders or no orders, I'm not letting this dog go," muttered one of Leon's captors.

"Bring him then, and we'll hang him proper later."

Noel scooted closer as they force-marched the struggling Leon toward a horse. Leon was cursing them furiously, fear evident in his voice.

"Fool," mouthed Noel, well aware of what he'd tried to do. He was so appalled by how closely Leon had come to killing Washington that he was tempted to let them take Leon away. But one form of disaster didn't justify another.

Noel made a running tackle for one of Leon's captors.

Leon went down, shoved hard in the man's surprise. Noel's weight should have borne the man to the ground, but he was a burly fellow, built like Gibraltar. He staggered but didn't fall. While Noel was still grabbing for a good hold on him, he twisted around and planted a punch deep into Noel's stomach. Noel doubled over, gasping, and the man's fist hit him in the jaw.

Stars spun in Noel's eyes as he went staggering, but he shook his head and fought back.

"Run, Leon!" he yelled, ducking another blow.

The other colonial seized him from behind, pinning his arms, and his opponent got in several deep hooks to Noel's midsection. His fists were like hammers, toughened by a lifetime of hard physical labor. Gritting his teeth, Noel curled up his legs and kicked out, knocking the man back. By then Leon was pulling the other man off Noel. Noel turned around and punched the man behind the ear, nearly breaking his knuckles but sending him down.

A fist socked into his kidney. Noel grunted in pain and stumbled. The fist slammed into him again. He collapsed, the world spinning, unable to breathe for the pain. Leon pulled the man off him, but by then others had appeared in the darkness. They grabbed Leon by the arms.

"Is he the one?"

"Aye! We'll hang him sure for daring to shoot at our general. Come on, lads!"

Rough hands dragged Noel up. "What about this one?"

"Kill him and be done. Let's go!"

The burly man standing over Noel pulled a knife and swung. A shot rang out in the darkness, and Noel's executioner made a soft, surprised grunt as he fell.

The others scattered. More shots rang out, and another man went down. The redcoats were charging now, yelling like Scotsmen, and the remaining conspirators ran for it. Leon was dragged away with them.

Lying half underneath the dead man, Noel was nearly trampled as the British soldiers surged past him. He lay still, trying not to cough, and when they were past he slowly, painfully pulled himself free.

It seemed suddenly, impossibly quiet. Noel crawled on his hands and knees, swayed, and fell facedown. He retched horribly, then felt a little better for it.

"Where are you?" whispered Sally's voice from the darkness. "Dear God, where have you gone?"

"Hush," whispered Noel back, and choked down a fit of coughing as he picked himself up again. He was wheezing for air, and his legs had no strength left in them. His adrenaline-based charge and the beating he'd taken had left him completely spent. He went staggering into the bushes and nearly stumbled into her.

She gripped his sleeve, inadvertently touching one of his burns. "You were mad to rush them that way. They nearly killed you."

"Someone saved me," said Noel, pulling free of her hands.

"I did," said a small, rather feeble voice.

Noel looked around, unable to see in the dark. "Robert?"

"Leave him alone right now. He's being sick in the bushes," said Sally.

"See how *you* feel when you kill your first man," retorted Robert.

"Enough," said Noel, wiping clammy perspiration from his brow. He wanted to be sick again. He wanted to lie down and let the world end. But there were others depending on him. He had to hang on. "We've got to get out of here."

"But surely now—"

"Sally," he said sharply, "this doesn't change anything for you. If you stay here, you'll be arrested for treason. And Robert too."

"No!" she gasped. "He's just a boy."

"He's man enough to shoot a gun," said Noel. "For which I thank him. But his age won't protect him. Now come on!"

"Yes, Sally, don't be stupid," said Robert.

"Horses," she said.

Noel glanced back at the stables. "We haven't a prayer of getting any. We'll have to walk."

"They'll comb every inch of this country," said Robert. "They're stirred up like hornets."

"No wonder," said Noel grimly. "We'll just have to outsmart them. Hurry!"

But although they got away, they could make no time. Sally's shoes were soon ruined, and Noel was so tired he was grateful for the slow pace she held them to.

"I'm sorry. I'm so stupid," she kept saying, angry at herself and mortified. "I shall get us caught."

"We can carry you," said Robert with more optimism than practicality.

"Never!" she said with scorn. Her teeth were chattering with cold, but she didn't complain. "I'll make it somehow. I—"

"Hush!" said Noel, hearing hoofbeats. "Another patrol."

Together they ducked into a thicket, waiting huddled together while riders swept by.

Crouched there with his chin on Sally's back, her hair fragrant near his nostrils, Noel felt himself dozing off. It was Robert who roused him.

"Sir!" he said, tugging at Noel's epaulet. "They've gone on. It's safe."

Noel dragged his head up. "Hmm? Yes."

He tried to get to his feet, but it was easier to just sit there and let the mists swallow him again.

"I think he's hurt, Sally," said Robert worriedly over him. "They beat him awfully hard."

"He was sick enough to start with," she replied. "This night air can only do his fever more harm."

Noel heard himself coughing. Pain sawed through his lungs and throat. He told himself he sounded pathetic and forced himself to his feet.

"Oh, sir, I'm sorry we got you into this," said Robert. "Do you think you can keep going? There's a family who'll take us in, if we can but get there."

"We can't put anyone else at risk," said Sally sharply. "We have no right."

"Sweet remorse from you now that there's a price on your head," retorted Robert. "I warned you—"

Noel parted them before they could get into an argument. "We'll put no one in danger, but we do need shelter, a fire, and warmer clothes. I suppose they'll hang Leon at dawn. If you know anyone, Robert, who can tell me where that will happen, I want to seek him out now."

"Indeed I—I don't, sir. I'm sorry. Do you really think they'll kill your brother?"

"I know it," said Noel grimly. "The only question is, can I get there to stop it."

"I suppose we cannot let them kill your brother," said Robert with a sigh. "But he did a most dishonorable thing, shooting in cold blood like that. I'd never credit it had I not seen it."

"My brother," said Noel grimly, "has no honor, no conscience, and no sense of shame."

"And still you would save him," said Sally.

Noel looked at her. "Wouldn't you if he were your brother?"

She drew in her breath sharply. "I thank God I have Robert instead. Oh, Robert, I'm sorry I've been so stupid."

"Here, don't cry now," said Robert, throwing Noel a look of appeal.

Noel put his arm around her, although it hurt him, and she gathered herself against his chest and wept in silence as they walked on slowly.

They followed the river that night since they could not cross it. Just before dawn they came to an unguarded footbridge and went over it. The rising sun found them at a snug farmstead, listening to the chickens crow. A young boy was outside, cutting firewood for the kitchen hearth. Noel and Sally hid themselves in a gully while Robert sneaked off to steal some eggs.

Sally was as tense as wire while he was gone. Her gaze never strayed from the buildings. Noel closed his eyes and let his exhaustion absorb him, yet he could not get comfortable. He was either cold or hot, the fever made his head swim, and it hurt so much to breathe that all he could do was wheeze.

"He is coming. He is coming," whispered Sally. "No one has seen him. There is no alarm. Oh, hurry. Hurry!"

Minutes later Robert came hurtling over the side of the gully, breathless but triumphant. He was carrying a cloth bundle in his arms and handed it to Sally with a wide grin.

"There," he said. "See if that's not better than any eggs."

She unwrapped the cloth, nearly spilling the contents in her amazement. "Why, Robert, here are johnnycakes and a tub of butter and ham and apples. How did you get so much?"

"It was all on the table in the kitchen and no one in sight, so I just popped in and wrapped up the tablecloth. They'll catch on in a minute so we'd better clear off."

In the distance there came a shout and voices raised in discovery. Robert grinned. "See?"

"You're enjoying yourself far too much," said Sally with mock severity. "You know what the Bible says about thievery."

There came a tug on Noel's uninjured hand. "Sir?" said Robert. "Sir, wake up."

"Not asleep," mumbled Noel without opening his eyes.

"Come, we can't stay here. I know you're tired, but you've got to get up."

"Go on," said Noel, coughing. Before, his LOC had always had emergency medical programming to help him if he got in trouble. It wasn't working, of course. Nothing was working. Between Leon and Qwip, home was out of reach. "Trapped," he said. "Finished."

"No, we *aren't* trapped, and we *aren't* finished," said Sally. She pulled Noel upright and helped Robert get him on his feet. "We owe you our lives and we aren't going to abandon you. Do try, please."

Her voice had long since lost its haughty tone. She sounded genuinely worried about him, and Noel tried to look into her eyes to see if she'd changed. But the sun dazzled him, and he couldn't see her face for the golden haze that shone over her. Behind her, another shape seemed to hover, watching.

He frowned, his wits coming back to him in anger. "Go away!" he said sharply. "Qwip, go away!"

Robert looked around in puzzlement. "Who's he talking to?"

She bit her lip and placed her hand upon Noel's hot cheek. "He's burning with fever. I fear for his reason."

"It's Qwip," said Noel, irritated with them for not understanding. "Don't worry about him. I can keep him away. It's Leon I can't save."

The sound of a cocked musket made them all freeze. Noel and the others looked up and saw a man with a grizzled beard standing over them on the bank. He held a gun pointed down at their heads.

"It's yourselves you should be thinking of saving," he said. "Thieves and a redcoat. Now that's a fine thing to find before a man's breakfast!"

At once Robert stepped in front of Noel. "If you please, sir. He's no redcoat."

"Got one on," said the man, squinting at them.

"It's—"

"Robert," said Noel and gently pushed him to one side.

"Well, sir!" said the man loudly. "Are you going to speak up for yourself? You're a soldier, are you not?"

Noel shook his head.

"Hah!" The man spat. "Deserter?"

Noel shook his head.

"Spy, then. Mangy thieving sneaks. I know the type, and I don't hold with 'em!"

"No, he's not a spy," said Robert hotly. "Stop being such a dolt and *listen*—"

"Be quiet," said Noel, and with a furious blush Robert held his tongue.

"Lad's a bit hot under the collar," said the man.

Robert stirred, and Noel put his hand on his shoulder and squeezed.

"The uniform is borrowed," said Noel.

"Aye, you're a spy all right. But on the right side, I gather. Now why'd you send that young 'un to steal my breakfast? Ain't you decent enough to come to a man's door and ask for food?"

"In a red uniform?" asked Noel.

A reluctant smile tugged at the corners of the man's mouth. He gnawed on his beard a moment, then nodded and lowered his musket a fraction. "I see your point. Well, bring it all back and the wife and me'll share with you."

With the danger over, things got foggy for Noel again. Robert and Sally bundled up the food and climbed out of the gully, pulling him with them. The farmer finally gave a hand, steadying Noel when he would have fallen.

"Whew, you're in a bad way, son."

"He swam the river and got an inflammation of the lungs," said Sally. "And now we've walked all night in the air."

"No, that's not good. Well, the wife's fair at nursing."

He led them to the house, where they were met by a plump woman with apple cheeks and a little bun on top of her head. Three small shy girls in pigtails peeped around her skirts.

"Well, Mrs. Kinkiddie!" he said loudly. "I've brought three vagrants to eat breakfast."

"So I see, Mr. Kinkiddie," she said in a grim voice. "Did you get our breakfast back?"

Robert held out the bundle. "Yes, ma'am," he said, his face bright red. "I'm sorry I took it. We were so hungry, you see."

Her brows shot up. "Oh? And how long has a morsel like yourself gone without food? A few hours? What of Washington's fine soldiers starving and dying over in the valley? What of poor folks who have to give all their cows and winter stores to the British? What of them? And you stealing from honest folks. Shame on you, boy."

"Now, now, no more of your scolding," said Kinkiddie. "The lad's sorry, and there's no harm done."

"No harm?" she said, her eyes snapping. "And me to serve a redcoat in my own home? I'll not do it! No, sir," she added to Noel. "For all you bring the whole regiment down on me. I won't do it."

"He's a sick man, wife!" bawled Kinkiddie. "Enough of your tongue. He's no redcoat for all he's got one on. Now set the table and act like a Christian."

"I see," she said, not giving ground. "He stands there in a uniform and tells you he's not one of them, and that's all you need to believe him? Well, sir, I—"

"Please," said Sally in a soft voice. "Please. He did it to help us escape. He's very sick, and I think if he stands much longer he'll faint."

"Sick?" cried Mrs. Kinkiddie in alarm. She drew her children closer to her. "And what has he brought into the house? Plague? Smallpox?"

"Ah!" said Kinkiddie in disgust. Stomping into the house past her, he stood his musket in a corner and sat down at the table. "He swam the river and took sick in his lungs. Now give over, woman, and set out my breakfast!"

Mrs. Kinkiddie blinked and seemed to find herself with no more accusations. "Well, then," she said at last. "Come to the fire. I'll see what's to be done."

Sally, Robert, and Noel gathered gratefully around the fire roaring on the hearth. Sally shook out her cloak and smoothed the wrinkles in her satin skirt.

"What a dreadful woman," she whispered, "although I think he means to be kind."

"She's just scared," said Noel, wheezing. He sat on the floor and leaned his shoulder against the wall. "Can't blame her."

"At least you can get warm here," said Sally, smoothing back his hair.

"Well?" yelled Kinkiddie. "It's on the table. Come and eat it."

Robert took Noel's elbow, but Noel shook his head with a faint smile. "Not hungry, boy. Go on."

"But, sir, you must keep up your strength."

Noel closed his eyes, and heard Sally urging Robert away.

He wasn't sure if it was the hissing and roaring of the fire or the fever drumming in his ears. He sank into the sound, depressed and sick at heart. By now the men must have read some pronouncement over Leon. They would have bound his hands behind him and hoisted him onto a horse. The noose would have been placed over his head. He would have sneered, as he always did, cowardice and fear shining in his eyes. Someone would have whipped the horse on the rump, startling it forward, and Leon would be swinging now, swinging in the cold spring wind, his feet kicking for a moment, then all still. Would they leave him hanging there, a testament to others who would dare try infamy? Or would they cut him down and bury him?

Did creatures duplicated in a process that violated physics go somewhere when they died? Through the centuries the church had worried over men who had lost their souls. What became of men who never had souls at all?

Noel slipped deeper into the warmth surrounding him. He was comfortable now. His aches and bruises seemed far away. As long as he didn't try to breathe deeply, even his chest didn't hurt as much. In a way, it was almost a comfort, knowing now that the game was finished. He couldn't take Leon back to the Institute. The anomaly would never be closed. The time loop would circle for all eternity. He would stay here, trapped in the past, for there was nowhere else to go.

It wasn't so bad, now that matters had been taken from his hands. It wasn't so bad, giving up.

It wasn't so bad, letting go.

CHAPTER 14

Qwip came to visit him, in the place of between.

The translucent image of bald head, pointed ears, and smooth oval face hung over Noel like a curtain, ever shifting, never constant.

"I am curious," said Qwip.

"About what?"

"What is the sensation of dying?"

The question was irritating. "Why ask me?" retorted Noel.

"They say that is what you are doing."

"Who says so?"

"The creatures who surround you."

Noel opened his eyes very wide and looked, but he saw nothing but Qwip. He didn't like Qwip. He wished he would go away. "I don't see anyone," he said.

"The creatures who surround your corporeal form," said Qwip, "at coordinates 4060—"

"I don't want to hear about coordinates," said Noel. "I don't like you. Go away."

"But I am curious."

"About death?"

"Yes. This is termination?"

"Of course it is. You threatened me with it the first time we met."

"But this is a sadness to the creatures. They have not instructed your termination."

"No, I think that came from your side," said Noel dryly. "So I'm dying." It did not seem to matter very much. He could consider the whole thing abstractly. "It's not like I expected."

"What do you expect? Do you think about termination prior to the event itself? You are a peculiar creature."

"So're you," said Noel. He closed his eyes, but Qwip didn't leave. Noel sighed and raised his head. "What are you, a candidate for mortuary school? I don't want to talk about it."

"I am not to blame," said Qwip. "I was instructed to terminate you if you did not comply with the terms of your agreement. I have not carried out my instructions. The matter is not closed, yet you die. Explain."

"Well, it just happens sometimes," said Noel with sarcasm. "Elephants do it too. Only they get to go off by themselves and die in peace."

"Elephants?"

"Yeah. You'd like them."

"Are they in another alternate dimension?"

Noel tried not to laugh. "Yeah, that's where they are all right. You could go look for them."

"I would rather discuss information with you."

"It's a very boring subject."

Qwip hovered over him, waiting.

Noel glared at him. "Don't you ever go home?"

"I do not understand that reference."

"Home equals your origin point. Go there."

"The matter is not closed. I have not carried out my instructions."

"Look, get this straight. I'm not going back to Chicago. I'm not going back to the Time Institute. I'm . . . not . . . going. Get it? The train has stopped, pal. And you can't go with me to see the future."

"I was curious about your future," Qwip said with something that sounded like regret.

"You don't belong in it."

"Why?"

"You just don't! How can you be so dense? When I nearly blundered into your dimension, all the warning bells went off, and they sent you out to attack me. I was threatened with termination, and I've been threatened with it ever since. Don't you remember all that?"

"Perfectly."

"And you don't see the correlation?"

"What correlation?"

Noel tried to sweep Qwip away, but he just swirled and re-formed like a vapor. "What goes for me, goes for you."

"Explain."

"You didn't want me to enter your dimension. I don't want you in mine."

"Why?"

"You are considered an intruder," said Noel between his teeth. "We would like to terminate you."

"You cannot terminate me," said Qwip. "It is not within the capabilities of your technology."

Noel snorted and said nothing.

"I ask questions because I wish to understand. To gather information is important. Please answer."

Noel said nothing.

"Please answer."

"Answer what, damn you?" said Noel.

"You wish to terminate me. You are . . . you are angry? Define angry."

"Angry is how I felt after you invaded my body."

"Possession is a means of control."

"Yeah? Well, I didn't like it."

"Explain."

"I didn't want you to do it."

"Why?"

"It was against my will."

Qwip's mouth opened for a moment. "Will?" he said. "Individual will?"

"Yes."

"A peculiar concept. I must consider it."

"And what do you have," sneered Noel, "an ant mentality?"

"I do not understand that reference."

"Let me explain. It's unflattering," said Noel.

"You remain angry."

"Damn right."

"I do not understand."

Noel lifted his head, all patience gone. "Look, if I'm dying, I'd like to do it in peace. Okay? Just go away."

"But the matter is not closed."

"It'll be closed when I'm gone."

"Define gone."

"Terminated!" shouted Noel.

"But I have not terminated you."

"And who put you in charge? I can die without you."

"Do you wish termination, Noel?" asked Qwip.

Noel was silent, fuming.

"Do you wish termination?"

He said nothing.

"Do you wish termination?"

Goaded, Noel snapped, "No, damn it, I don't!"

"Then resist."

"Why should I? You'll just have another go at me."

"My range has been increased, but I do not think they will allow me to enter your origin coordinates," said Qwip sadly. "I will inquire for permission to conduct additional exploration. If permission is denied, I will experience regret. Do you have a reference for regret?"

"Yeah, I think I can understand that." Noel glared at him. "Excuse me if *I* don't feel regret. And don't bother to ask your boss for permission because I'm not taking you anywhere. Now go pester someone else."

"It is aloneness here between," said Qwip. "I would question Subject Two, but it achieves no result. Subject Two never wishes to talk to me. I have tried, but Subject Two is most unpleasant. You talk to me, Noel."

"Who," said Noel impatiently, "is Subject Two?"

"The inverse of Subject One."

"Gee, that tells me a lot," said Noel. "Who is Subject One?"

Qwip opened his mouth. "You are."

Noel frowned, sorting through it with lethargy. "The inverse of . . . you mean Leon?"

"A constant inversion, even in personality designations," said Qwip.

"You *do* mean Leon." Noel forgot his irritation and felt suddenly alert. "Is he alive? No, he can't be. I know he was terminated. So what happened to him after—after—well, is he here between?"

"This information pleases you," said Qwip slowly.

"Just answer my question."

"But I do not understand. There are many questions. All contradictory. Subject Two—"

"Leon," broke in Noel. "If you can call me Noel, you can call him Leon."

"I call you Noel as a gesture. It is to please you."

"Then please me by calling him Leon!"

Qwip wavered and almost started to vanish, then came back. "Agreed."

"Thank you," said Noel, exhausted by his anger. "So what's so hard about what I asked you? Is Leon here between?"

"No. Leon is not between."

"But his consciousness is somewhere. You said you tried to talk to him, so he's still—"

"Please, I have no references for this. Leon is at similar coordinates to your corporeal form."

Noel stared at him and slowly rose to a sitting position. He reached out his hand and tried to grip Qwip with his fingers, although Qwip was as thin as air. "Are you saying he's alive? That they didn't hang him?"

"Leon has not been terminated."

Noel dropped back and laughed. "Not terminated?"

"No, this has not occurred. That is why I do not understand your behavior. Why do you die?"

Noel was still smiling. "Why indeed?" he murmured.

Lashed to a horse, his bound hands swollen from lack of circulation, Leon ducked another tree branch and fumed. They were trotting through a forest, having left the road to avoid another British patrol. Bounced and jolted, his body aching from where they had beaten him earlier, Leon's patience had long ago run out. He'd tried manipulating the minds of his captors but they were too emotionally charged to pay heed to him. That angered him further. He'd cursed them, and they hit him. One of them tied a dirty handkerchief across his mouth to gag him.

More than once they'd dismounted among the trees and hidden while the British rode by. The men held the nostrils of their horses to keep them from whinnying. Someone held a cocked pistol at the back of Leon's skull to keep him from trying anything. Now and then one of the men would simply look at him, and Leon could sense fresh rage boiling up. The man would hit him hard, sometimes more than once, just because he'd tried to kill Washington.

Furious, Leon wanted to crush them all. But his own sense of cunning preserved him from being that foolhardy. Even if he knocked them all unconscious with the power of his mind, that would still leave him trussed and helpless. No, he had to bide his time and separate them.

He singled out the man who seemed to be giving most of the orders. "Split up," he whispered to the man's mind.

He kept sending that suggestion, and it kept being ignored. Leon wanted to scream with frustration. What were they so angry about? What were they so scared of? The British couldn't find them in the dark. Washington was safe. Leon's shot had missed. No harm had been done.

He tried to suggest that to their minds, but they were too upset to receive it.

Finally, just before dawn when Leon was frozen stiff in the saddle and his hands had gone completely numb, they drew rein at a crossroads.

"Time to split up," said the leader. "If we don't report for duty, Von Steuben will see our heads roll."

"What about our prisoner?" asked the man who held Leon's reins.

"Better do him quick, if we're to have a chance at all," said one of the others.

No, thought Leon at all of them. *No.*

"Not now. There's no time to do it properly," said the leader.

Leon's guard laughed. "Properly! Who the hell cares? He ought to get what's coming to him. An eye for an eye—"

"He'll get it all right," said the leader darkly. "But I want to let him stew in his own juices. Let him think it over before we execute him."

"The general said to let him go."

"The general's got a good heart, too good for the likes of this dog," said the leader. "Perkins, you take our prisoner over to the abandoned mill and keep him there. We'll say we got split up in the confusion and don't know what's become of you. See?"

Perkins grinned evilly, showing several missing teeth. "I see."

"We'll come back tonight and give him a trial."

"I can have a little fun in the meantime, can't I?" asked Perkins, still grinning.

The other two exchanged glances. "Mind you don't kill him before we get a chance to help you," said one.

"That's right," said the leader. "You keep him alive."

"Oh, he'll be alive." Perkins caught Leon's eye and removed his tricorn. He was missing his hair in front, and his skull was covered with a mass of red, terrible scars. "Half-scalped, I was, as a kid," he told Leon. "When I got better, I learned myself how to do it." He pulled out a wicked-looking knife. "I keep this sharp, all the time."

Leon stared at him, and swallowed hard.

"Don't scalp him till we get there," said the leader. "If he's messed up too much, he won't know we're hanging him. I want him *scared* of the rope, not grateful for it."

"Aw," said Perkins, disappointed, "it's too hard you are."

"There's other parts to skin," suggested the third man slyly. He and Perkins laughed, and the leader shook his head.

"I tell you, hold off until we come. You got that, Perkins?"

"Yes, sir," said Perkins sullenly. He executed a sloppy salute, then glanced at Leon and winked.

In other circumstances Leon might have considered him a kindred spirit, but not now, not after the hitting, the jabbing, the too-tight ropes. Leon eyed him darkly, waiting for an opportunity.

The two men rode off and with a tug on the reins, Perkins led Leon deeper into the forest. Leon waited until the men were far from sight or hearing. He waited until Perkins led him up to a deserted grist mill. Part of the place had burned some time ago, from the looks of the charred timbers and overgrowth. The huge wooden wheel still hung poised over the stream below. Leon could hear the rush of water.

He concentrated, gathering all the evil strength inside himself to reach past Perkins's darkness.

Perkins dismounted and ambled off to relieve himself. Then he returned, whistling tunelessly under his breath. Beneath his uniform his shirt was grimy. He hadn't shaved in several days. The stink of him filled the crisp morning air.

Untie my hands.

Perkins squinted up at Leon and pulled him bodily off the horse. Leon went tumbling to the ground and landed hard on his side. He barely choked back a cry.

Chuckling, Perkins kicked him. "On your feet."

Leon gnawed on the dirty gag and glared at him.

Perkins kicked him again. "On your feet."

Leon squirmed around in the dirt and could not get his feet under him.

"Come on, come on," said Perkins impatiently. He drew his knife and pressed the sharp tip to Leon's back, right above his bound hands.

Leon felt a small trickle of his blood course down his spine.

Perkins poked harder. "I could slice right through your backbone with this blade, then your legs wouldn't work. Or I could cut your hamstrings, and you'd never run again." He touched the back of Leon's knee, and Leon flinched. Perkins laughed. "Or, I could take some of your hair."

He gripped the hair at the back of Leon's skull. "Nice and black it is. I could say I took it off an Indian. Then the officers wouldn't care as much."

Leon cried out against the gag, and Perkins released him with a contemptuous shove of his face into the dirt.

"Aw, you're a dirty, yellow-livered coward, is all. Mewing and whimpering. I want a good scream from you."

Then take off the gag.

Cold metal touched Leon's cheek. He flinched, rolling his eyes to see the wide blade of the knife pressed against the side of his face. With a rapid flick, the knife sliced through the rag, and Leon spat it out.

Perkins kicked him in the ribs. "Scream, redcoat!"

Leon wanted to scream but with fury, not fear. This man was as cunning as he, as ruthless as he, as evil as he. He could not penetrate Perkins's sense of purpose, which was to inflict as much pain on him as possible.

For a moment Leon was tempted to negotiate, to plead. Then he caught himself up short. Was he mad? That was exactly the sort of thing Noel would attempt, and he was not Noel. He would never be Noel.

Self-disgust choked him. He had been contaminated when he had shared thoughts with Noel. To think he had actually taken pity—pity—on Noel and helped him. It was nauseating.

I am evil, he thought, focusing on all the old hatred to bring it back. *I am dark. I am wicked. I take pleasure in destroying what others want. And, Perkins, I am worse than you!*

He raised up, lifting himself by sheer effort of will. And he aimed all the blackened rot of himself at Perkins.

The man stopped in the act of kicking him again. His eyes went very wide and glassy. The knife dropped from his fingers. He staggered back, making a choking sound. Then he dropped dead.

Panting, Leon sagged to his knees. Great drops of sweat rolled off his forehead and splattered on the ground. He gulped in lungful after lungful of air, but as the tumult inside him quieted, he began to smile just a little to himself. That final moment of panic in Perkins's breast . . . how sweet to savor.

Leon flung back his hair from his eyes and staggered to his feet. Only then did he scowl with annoyance. For his hands were still tied, and Perkins was dead. Well, no matter. He had the knife. He would manage.

And he did.

After that it was agony, pacing about and swearing to himself as the circulation returned slowly to his swollen hands. He splashed his way into the stream and plunged his hands into the icy cold water. Gradually the swelling went down, and he was able to wiggle his fingers without discomfort. His skin resumed its normal color.

Leon then set to work. He changed his red uniform for Perkins's blue one. He examined Perkins's grimy papers and kept those too. With his British uniform rolled up and stowed in the saddlebags, he now had two identities. He started to untie the horse, then paused with his head cocked to one side.

He was remembering all the threats he had heard through the long night. He was remembering how Perkins had threatened to scalp him. He was remembering how they planned to hang him, gibbering and wetting himself in his terror.

Leon's lips drew back from his teeth. Why not give these barbarians a taste of something really scary?

He walked back to the corpse and lashed the feet together. For a moment he considered scalping what was left of Perkins's greasy hair, but that seemed far too tame. Instead, he decapitated the body. With a rope that he found in the unburned part of the mill, he hung the body upside down from a walnut tree. Blood began to sluggishly drain onto the ground. The head he tossed into the stream and watched as it bobbed and rolled in the water, carried away to shock some unsuspecting farmer downstream. With a stick he scratched Perkins's name in the dirt to help the man's friends identify him.

Smirking to himself, Leon drove his new knife into the ground several times to clean it. Then as he mounted the horse and rode away, he tipped back his head with a shout of laughter. Let these rustic buffoons have a taste of real atrocity and see how they liked it.

After nearly two weeks of roaming the countryside, robbing travelers and robbing homes, Leon was ready for a different kind of amusement. It was easy enough to ride up to a farm, scan the minds inside to see if they were sympathetic to the American or the British cause, don the appropriate uniform, and be greeted with an invitation to supper. But there was no challenge in that. He had discarded the idea of returning to Major Burton. Playing soldier had become a bore. Especially since Noel had interfered with his plans.

He did not think of Noel often, but when he did it was with a laugh. His stupid twin had not wanted to believe that they were finally entrenched in the past, but it was true. Leon had never stayed anywhere this long. Unlike before, Noel had not turned up to stop his activities. It was most liberating.

But it was becoming a bore too.

Leon had begun to wonder in the back of his mind if jumping from time to time wasn't more exciting than plodding along every day in the same stretch of backward culture.

But he wasn't ready to admit it and he decided to invent a different kind of game for himself.

Noonday found him stretched out atop a knoll with his hands cupped around his eyes to shield them from the sun. He watched a small train of supply wagons laboring along a muddy road. Continental troops rode guard. They looked nervous, as well they should, slinking through country that was primarily British controlled.

Leon mounted and rode down the hill behind them. Instead of catching up with them, he circled a half mile or so around and got ahead of them. Then swinging onto the road, he kicked his horse to a brisk trot and met the vanguard.

The officer in charge was young and handsome, with a plume in his tricorne and a crimson sash to hold his sword. He threw up his hand and halted the company before riding ahead a few paces to meet Leon.

His dark eyes were intelligent and searching. They observed the lather on Leon's horse, the mud splattered across Leon's uniform.

He frowned in quick concern. "Hello, Corporal. Something amiss?"

Leon scanned the surface thoughts of the soldier's mind rapidly. *Ambush . . . weary horses . . . army pay to be protected . . .* Leon couldn't help but glance down the line. The next-to-last wagon held the payroll, the first script the Continental troops had probably been paid all winter. Everything else was blankets, food, and clothing . . . the usual boring supplies.

"Something amiss?" repeated the officer.

"Yes, sir," said Leon urgently. He caught another layer of thought: *First command . . . must look good . . . heavy responsibility . . . mustn't fail the general.* Leon almost smiled and stopped himself just in time. "Trouble ahead."

"I was afraid of that. Things have been going too well. I'm surprised you didn't bring troops with you."

"That's the trouble," said Leon. "They're holding the British at the next crossroads. I broke away to give you the warning."

The lieutenant frowned and tried his best not to look alarmed. "How much time?"

"Not much."

"Good lord." The lieutenant pulled a worn map from his saddlebags and spread it across his knee. "We're here, I think."

Leon examined the map. It was full of crooked country roads, crisscrossing everywhere. He traced a route with his finger. "They're here. My company can't hold them long. I was given orders to turn you east, then north. You see? This way."

"Right," said the lieutenant with decision. He turned around in the saddle and bawled orders.

Within minutes the wagons were turning ponderously back the way they'd come, the large wooden wheels rolling with great smacking slurps of the mire. They were using oxen to draw them, instead of horses. The beasts lowed in complaint, and the drivers swore and cracked their whips.

Leon trotted his horse up and down, making sure his orders added to the general confusion. When they were at last stretched out and going again, the payroll wagon was last in line, and the bulk of the troops riding guard had been positioned somewhere near the middle. Leon placed himself at the rear, constantly urging the men on and trying not to gloat.

By dusk they were lost. The lieutenant was peering over his map by lantern light and two of his subordinates were arguing. Leon found the driver of his target wagon to be very dull-witted and almost impossible to reach. He simplified his suggestions.

"You're sleepy."

The driver yawned and scratched his belly.

"Very sleepy."

The driver yawned so enormously Leon heard his jaws pop.

"So sleepy you cannot stay awake. Better to let someone else hold the reins. Drop the reins. Drop the reins. Go to sleep."

Finally the driver's head nodded. He snored.

Leon wheeled his horse in front of the team. The oxen stopped willingly.

The driver ahead glanced back. "Problem?"

"No, but I think this man's been drinking whiskey on the sly," said Leon. "He's passed out. I'll take the reins."

Tying his horse to the wagon, Leon climbed onto the seat and urged the team forward. As the shadows lengthened and they lost the daylight, he let the wagon fall behind. He cast his mind at the men ahead of him.

"The last wagon is right behind you. Close and safe. Don't look back. We're all close together."

Halting the team when it was too dark for them to see him, Leon jumped into the back and flipped back the tarp. He found bags of mail for the soldiers and kicked them aside with contempt. The money chest itself was too heavy to carry. Drawing his knife, he used the stout blade to pry open the lock. For a moment he thought he would break the blade, then the lock released and he threw back the lid.

He had to explore by feel rather than sight. At first all he touched were order pouches, then paper. Disappointment welled up in his throat. The cheapskates. Small wonder they were losing the war if they used worthless paper for money. Then in the bottom he found hard coinage. He lifted out the clinking bags and tucked them into his pockets, breathing fast and chuckling to himself.

When he had all he could carry, he heard a shout up ahead. Unwilling to press his luck further, Leon jumped from the wagon. The weight he was carrying made him fall. It took him a moment to lever himself upright. Then he staggered to his horse. He could not mount. The gold was holding him down. Swearing under his breath, he took out some of it and threw it on the ground.

He had hauled himself halfway into the saddle when he heard hoofbeats coming fast. Swinging his leg over, he sawed at the reins, making his horse rear, and reached for his pistol.

A lantern was opened, casting light suddenly into his eyes. Blinded, Leon wheeled his horse around. Another lantern shone at him.

"Stand where you are!" said the lieutenant in ringing tones. "What's this wagon doing so far behind? Why is the driver unconscious?"

The light shone closer. Leon squinted and slipped his thumb across the hammer of his pistol.

"Bring your hands out where we can see them," said the lieutenant.

"It's the payroll wagon, sir," said the sergeant grimly. "He's somehow switched it to the rear. While we were maneuvering, I've no doubt."

"Nor I," said the lieutenant. He gazed at Leon with eyes of steel. "Dismount, Corporal, and turn out your pockets."

"The hell I will," snarled Leon and fired.

Almost simultaneously someone shot back. Leon missed, and a streak of fire branded his arm. He gasped and reeled, clutching himself. There was blood, his blood, flowing freely. He could feel the heat of it upon his fingers. The salty wetness of it stank in his nostrils.

"Get him down," said the lieutenant angrily.

Rough hands pulled Leon off his horse and held him fast. They searched him, pulling out the gold.

"The penalties for robbing army payroll are very severe, Corporal," said the lieutenant. "Did you really think you could pull off something like this?"

Leon squinted up at him with contempt. "Nearly did it, didn't I?"

The sergeant struck him. "You will address the lieutenant with respect."

Leon touched his sore lip with the tip of his tongue. "Sir," he added with more insolence than ever.

"Sergeant, here're his papers," said one of the men who searched him.

The sergeant examined them, then passed them to the lieutenant.

"Corporal Edward Perkins," he said.

"Naw!" said a voice in rough protest.

Leon jerked against the hands holding him, but his guards only tightened their grip. A private pushed his way forward and spat.

"That ain't never Ned Perkins."

"You know the man?" asked the lieutenant in astonishment.

"Aye, sir. That I do. Served with him against the injuns. And him a scurvy, pox-ridden scoundrel as ever was."

The sergeant glared at Leon. "Seems to describe this man well enough."

"Well, he ain't Perkins. Ain't I just been saying so?"

The lieutenant frowned. "What is your true name?"

Leon said nothing.

"Where did you get these papers?"

Again Leon said nothing. He tried to touch the lieutenant's mind, but now it was closed tight against him with anger and steely contempt.

"A deserter most like," said the sergeant.

They went through the saddlebags, and the sergeant whistled. "Look at this, sir! A British uniform."

The scarlet cloth looked like blood in the lantern light. The lieutenant examined Leon's British papers. "A commissioned lieutenant in His Majesty's army, Leon Nardek." He glanced up, his eyes searching and hard. "Is that your true name?"

In spite of himself Leon nodded.

The men holding his arms gave them a twist that made him gasp. "A bloody redcoat."

"Worse, a spy and a thief. Perhaps a murderer as well," said the lieutenant grimly. "It's certain you didn't come honestly by the uniform you're wearing."

"Now, Lieutenant," said Leon placatingly, seeking a sliver of an opening, any hint of an opportunity to strike the young officer's thoughts, "surely we can—"

"Take this man away and put him in shackles," said the lieutenant. "He is the worst kind of villain, and will be dealt with as soon as we reach headquarters. Sergeant, turn these wagons around."

"And what of the British trying to waylay us, sir?"

The lieutenant's face was a grim mask. He gazed at Leon with absolutely no mercy. "I believe that was only a ploy to delay and confuse us. Turn the wagons, now, and be sharp about it!"

"Wait," said Leon. "Lieutenant, we should discuss this like civilized men."

"I don't believe you know the meaning of the term," said the lieutenant icily.

And Leon was taken away.

CHAPTER 15

Bright, uncomfortable sunlight on Noel's face awakened him. Squinting, he shifted his head to avoid it, and found the pillow lumpy and full of quills that tried to stick him through the cloth.

"Feathers," he said, very distinctly, and opened his eyes wide.

He saw that he was in a bed, tucked beneath a low ceiling. Sally, dressed in frumpy brown homespun, sat beside him. She had been reading, but when he spoke she dropped the book and stared at him with a dawning smile.

"You're awake," she said. "Do—do you know me?"

He smiled back. His facial muscles felt stiff as though they hadn't moved in a long time. "Sally Crewe," he said in a voice that sounded like a rusty hinge.

"Praise God," she said. "Let me get you some water."

She bustled around him then, turning his pillow and smoothing out the lumps. She fetched him a glass of water and supported his head while he drank it. She pulled open the curtains and let even more sunlight in. She took his hand in hers and held it.

"Oh, yes, your skin is cool. The fever is gone, and your breathing is much easier. Are you hungry?"

He realized that he was ravenous. He nodded.

"I'll tell Mrs. Kinkiddie. Just rest and I'll be back right away."

She rushed out.

Noel frowned at the room. He'd never seen it before, and couldn't imagine how he'd come here. Things seemed a little crooked, a little out of perspective. He felt as though he'd been away a long time.

Slowly he sat up, although his arms were absurdly weak and trembled when he tried to support himself. His face was covered with beard, and that shocked him. How long had he been here? Travel slowed beard growth. Most of the time, shaving was never necessary at all. For that effect to have worn off, he must have been here . . .

He flung back the covers. Beneath his nightshirt, his legs were skeleton thin and pale. He could count every rib. Naturally lean, he had dropped weight to skin and bones.

Outside birds were singing merrily. He stared at the window, frowning for a long time before his conscious brain registered what his senses were telling him.

There were green leaves outside the glass.

Green leaves.

Not buds, but leaves. How many days, how many weeks had he lain here? It wasn't possible.

He pushed himself out of bed and tottered two steps before he fell. Slowly he righted himself again and stood there clinging to the bedpost.

"Sir, you're up!" called out Robert in surprise.

The boy came charging in with his shirt sleeves rolled up and his jerkin covered with dust. A huge grin covered his face. "Sally said you were awake, but I didn't expect to see you out of bed. Don't you think you'd better get back in?"

"No," said Noel. "How long have I been here?"

"Going on three weeks, and fair worried we've been, I can tell you. Jupiter, you've been sick. We thought you were going to die."

"Oh?" Noel put his arm around the boy's shoulders and let him help him back to bed. "That sounds familiar."

"Well, you talked about dying a lot. I guess you were upset about your brother."

Noel frowned. "Leon."

"Yes, well, anyway," said Robert, hurrying past that subject, "the way you raved when the fever had you—you said the most fantastic things."

"What things?" asked Noel worriedly. He was prohibited from using modern terminology that might betray his origins.

"Well, you talked of elephants, sir."

Noel grinned. "Did I?"

"And there was a man that you talked to. I don't think you liked him much for you were always telling him to go away. Sometimes you would strike out at him. And swear."

"Did I scorch your sister's ears?"

"No, I don't think so," said Robert with a grin. "She can swear pretty good herself if she's mad enough."

"What else?"

"None of the rest made any sense at all. You were reliving old memories sometimes, bad ones, some of them."

Noel nodded and leaned back against his pillows. "Three weeks," he said, still amazed. But there was a hollowness growing inside him. He must be completely cut off from all contact with the time portal. He had dropped into the past beyond the Institute's reach.

He looked down at his hands. His LOC was missing. He clenched his fingers. "My LOC!" he said in horror.

"What? Your locket, did you say?"

Noel shook his head, trying to still his rising panic. "I was wearing a ring. It's—"

"Don't worry," said Robert, fishing out a string from inside his shirt. The ring hung on it. "I've been keeping it safe for you. Sally and Mr. Kinkiddie took it off. They were afraid your hand wouldn't heal properly."

He slipped the string off over his head and pressed the ring into Noel's hand. "There it is, sir. Safe and sound. We didn't lose it."

Noel let out his breath in relief and gripped the LOC tightly in his fist. It was still with him. He still had a chance to get home. Things were okay. Recall hadn't worked because they took off the LOC. That was all.

"Okay," he said shakily. "Okay."

"No one stole it," said Robert gently. "Indeed, we took the greatest care to keep it safe. I'm sorry I upset you—"

"Robert?" said Sally in concern. "Upset him? How? What have you been doing?"

She came in briskly, carrying a tray. "Good heavens, Mr. Kedran. You don't look half as well as when I left you."

Noel looked up distractedly. "I'm okay."

"You're as white as the sheets. Here's some broth. It's hot and very good."

She picked up a spoon, but Noel reached out for it. He wasn't going to be fed like a baby.

"You mustn't tire yourself. If you overdo, your fever could come back."

As hungry as he was, Noel wanted to be alone so he could question his LOC. Was it even working? He had to know.

"I can feed myself," he said.

"I'm sure you can, but why don't you taste this first?"

So he had to lie there and be spoon-fed. The soup needed salt, but it tasted fine to a starving man. When the bowl was less than half-empty, he found himself abruptly too full and tired to continue.

"Enough for now, I think," said Sally. "Do you feel strong enough for a shave?"

It was tempting. His whole face itched. He couldn't remember when he'd ever had a beard. He wanted it off, but other things had to come first.

He feigned a yawn.

"Perhaps another nap now," she said with a smile. "Then we'll take off that fine dark growth, unless you're of a mind to keep it?"

"No!" he said in revulsion.

She cleared the tray off the bed and gave him a little curtsy. "Enjoy your nap, sir. I'll check on you later."

Shooing Robert ahead of her, she closed the door.

As soon as they were gone, chattering to each other as they went downstairs, Noel struggled out of bed. He staggered to the door, as weak as a newborn kitten, and put the chair under the latch. By the time he got back into bed, he was out of breath and ready to collapse with fatigue. He rested a moment, then slipped the ring on. It was too big now since he'd lost weight. He clenched his hands to keep them from shaking.

"LOC," he said, almost afraid to say the words, "activate."

At first nothing happened at all, then with a little hiccup and whir the blue light flashed across his hand. "On-line," said the LOC. "One moment for self-test . . . ready."

Noel wiped his forehead. "You're working."

"Affirmative."

He tipped back his head with a chuckle. "Thank God. We are back!"

"No travel has commenced since initial materialization at these coordinates."

"Absolutely." Noel forced himself to be sober, although a grin kept tugging at the corners of his mouth. "Okay, down to business. Have you managed self-repairs?"

"Specify."

"All damaged areas."

"Negative. Molecular shift parameters remain off—"

"Stop. I don't care what you look like. Have you repaired the recall sequence function?"

The LOC flashed steadily. "Repairs ran past initial estimate of seven point two three hours."

"You might say my repairs ran overtime too," said Noel.

"Recall function has been rerouted. Accuracy loss is predicted at ninety-seven point nine nine percent."

Noel blinked. "About two points off? What does that mean? We'll miss the time portal?"

"The possibility exists. Two point—"

"Stop. I don't like statistics. If we're in the time stream, how can we miss the portal?"

"According to the first principle of interdimensional dynamics, the Sheffield curve must intersect with—"

"Stop," said Noel hastily. "Never mind. I'm still willing to take the risk."

"Affirmative."

Noel thought he heard a noise and stopped, listening. The sound did not come again. After a while he relaxed and scrunched lower beneath the covers.

"I need information and fast," he said, lowering his voice. "First, search biographies for Sally or Robert Crewe, circa 1778."

"Scanning . . . Robert Mathias Crewe, governor of Pennsylvania 1798–1802, married Annabel Brewster of Philadelphia and had two sons, Noel Robert Crewe and John Lester Crewe."

Noel stared in astonishment. "My God. Quick, have there been any alterations to history? Any problems?"

"Negative. The history of Robert Crewe is unchanged."

A smile widened across Noel's face. "So he's going to name his oldest son after me? The little devil."

"The sons of Robert Crewe founded the Independence Bank of Philadelphia, later part of the funding consortium of DIONEK Consolidated, famous in the twenty-third century for—"

"Stop. Okay, Robert is fine. What about Sally?"

"I scan no information for Sally Crewe."

Noel's good mood vanished. "Nothing? Try, uh, Sarah."

"Negative for this date and location."

Noel propped himself up on one elbow and scratched his beard. "Cross-reference with Robert. There must be some information about her."

"Scanning."

This was it, Noel told himself. This was where his accidental interference had changed history. It always happened. Getting involved with people had too many ramifications.

"Data banks are incomplete," said the LOC. "Reference to one S. Crewe, spinster, in household of Robert Crewe."

"That's her." Noel frowned. "A spinster? Don't you have anything else?"

"Data banks are incomplete."

Spinster. Noel knew that originally the word referred to an unmarried woman of the household. Later it came to have the connotations of failure attached to it, as though a woman who did not marry somehow came short of what society, her relatives, and destiny had intended. Finally the word fell out of usage altogether. But he found himself thinking about lovely Sally Crewe as he had first seen her, so self-assured, so spirited, so beautiful. What kind of future was she to have? What kind of life would she live? A happy one? A bitter, disappointed one? Compression into one tiny historical footnote as S. Crewe, spinster, conveyed no information at all.

"She deserves more than that," said Noel. Then he put his thoughts in the context of the times in which Sally lived. A woman married or she did not. If she did not, she was cared for and served as a dutiful aunt, worked for charity, and stayed behind the scenes. If she married, she could look forward to one pregnancy after another, without benefit of medical attention. She could see half or more of her children die from childhood diseases, or she could die herself from childbirth fever. He shuddered, unable to imagine Sally in any of those scenarios. Maybe being a spinster wasn't so bad after all.

"Please specify instructions," said the LOC.

He sighed. "No instructions. Does her history change? Any problems there?"

"Unknown. No indications of alteration."

"You mean I don't affect their lives at all? Other than having a son named after me?"

"Affirmative."

"That's a relief," said Noel, but he couldn't help feel a bit deflated. "What about the people who live here? The, uh, Kinkiddles. No, the Kinkiddies."

"Negative," said the LOC.

"No alterations?"

"This entry is not in my data banks."

"Then I'm not going to worry about them. Okay, now for the important question. Leon."

"Specify instructions."

"Can—can you locate him?"

"Negative."

Everything in Noel grew very still. "Is he dead?"

"Negative."

"Are you malfunctioning? Or is that an informed response?"

"No malfunction."

"If you don't know where he is, how do you know he wasn't hanged?"

The LOC did not immediately answer. "Contradictory questions. I have relayed no information about hangings."

"No, I asked if he was dead."

"Negative."

"How do you know?"

"Scanning is possible."

"Then you *do* have his location?"

"Negative."

Noel struck the bed with his fist. "I don't understand. Do you know where he is, or don't you?"

"Negative."

"But you can scan him?"

"Affirmative."

"Why can't you get a fix on his location?"

The LOC flashed. "Unknown."

"Find out. Run diagnostics if necessary."

The LOC hummed to itself a moment. Noel heard that tiny hiccuping sound and a whir. He frowned, worry creeping over him. Those were not normal operating noises.

"Error corrected," announced the LOC.

"Great. Now tell me where he is."

"Coordinates—"

"Stop. Translate to town or landmark."

"Headquarters of Continental Army. Valley Forge."

Noel rolled his eyes. "Swell. How am I going to get him out of there?"

"Four courses of action can be given in logical order of priority—"

"Stop. No thanks. I'll figure out something for myself. What's our recall deadline?"

"Scanning . . . no deadline."

"What?"

"No deadline."

Noel shook his head. "That's impossible."

"No deadline."

"What's happened to safety-chain programming, antirogue programming, automatic functions?"

"Canceled."

Noel was stunned. It had to be part of the damage. "Recall is no longer possible?" he asked in a voice that didn't even sound like his.

"Manual recall instructions only. Automatics not functioning."

"Damaged?"

The LOC flashed.

Noel forced himself to stay calm. "But we can still initiate recall sequence?"

"Affirmative. Voice command only."

"Okay, that works. Okay." He ran his fingers through his hair. "No recall deadline. That's incredible."

He backed off from the freedom of the idea, afraid of temptation. He'd been here nearly a month. Leon had been here even longer. Usually they managed to goof up history within minutes or hours.

"Postulation of history alterations can be given—"

"No!" said Noel hastily. "I don't even want to know."

"Conditioning implant has failed," said the LOC.

Noel rubbed his arm where the implant was located. "I guessed that. I could stay here, and there's no one to stop me."

"Affirmative."

"But I don't want to stay," said Noel. "I want to go home. I want to kick that anomaly back where it came from. I want Leon reassimilated so that he doesn't cause any more trouble. I want to see if my friends are okay."

He couldn't forget that he had left the Time Institute in major trouble, in danger of being shut down permanently. His friend Trojan was insane from a travel accident, and others had died.

And while time duration did not correlate on either side of the portal, Noel knew he did not have an indefinite amount of time to fix the problems he'd been sent back for. He and the other technicians had defied orders to open the time portal. If it was shut down again, he would never get back at all.

He sighed. "So it comes back to the same old thing. Find Leon and attempt return one more time."

"Affirmative."

Noel thought of something else. "LOC, can you scan for an entity called Qwip?"

"Specify Qwip."

"You ought to know," said Noel. "After all, Qwip caused that feedback problem during our last recall attempt. You had a meltdown and nearly took me with you."

"Specify Qwip."

Noel draped his hand over his eyes. There was no point in arguing with a literal-minded computer. "Qwip is a noncorporeal consciousness point from an alternate dimension. A door—no, a window—to that dimension has been opened by the distortions in the time stream. Qwip has reached through. Is that enough information?"

"Affirmative. Will scan."

"I want to know if Qwip is anywhere nearby."

The LOC said nothing.

Noel tapped the ring with his finger. "You working in there?"

"Affirmative."

"Any sign of Qwip?"

"Qwip is an energy force of—"

"I don't want a definition," said Noel impatiently. "I want you to keep a watch for him. If he shows up, alert me. Understood?"

The LOC hiccuped and whirred. "Affirmative."

"I don't want to be possessed again. If we're to achieve recall, we've got to keep Qwip away."

"Affirm—ative."

"LOC, are you malfunctioning?"

"Negative," said the LOC firmly.

"Run a self-check anyway."

"All systems in working order."

"You're sure?"

"Affirmative."

Noel's frown deepened. "Don't fail me now, buddy. I depend on you to get me out of this time. Okay?"

"Affirmative. Systems functioning."

"Good. Deactivate."

The blue light flashed and went out as the LOC shut down. Noel studied the ring on his finger for a long while, troubled more than he wanted to admit. There was a good chance that the LOC still had a glitch in its programming. It probably had more than one, and he couldn't rely on it to admit it if it did.

All the more reason to get back on his feet as quickly as possible. It was time to travel.

CHAPTER 16

Three days later, Noel was back on his feet, well enough in his own judgment to handle himself. Sally had tried to persuade him that he was rushing things. Mrs. Kinkiddie had scolded him for eating her out of house and home, for using up all her good linens and melting her kitchen with all the water heated for his nursing, and for making them worry so. He decided that the plump woman's bark was worse than her bite, but he was still ready to go.

"So anxious to be gone," murmured Sally as he walked with her after supper on the eve of his departure. "We've barely gotten a chance to talk with you, to enjoy your conversation and wit."

In the starlight her hair was a soft cloud about her face. Her slim white shoulders gleamed where her shawl had slipped down. Now and then he could see the glistening of her eyes or glimpse a touch of moonlight upon her cheek. She smelled of lavender, and as she walked beside him—straight and graceful—all he could think about was her fate, to go through life unloved, unclaimed, unwanted. He wished suddenly that he could take her back with him instead of Leon.

How ironic life was, how unfair sometimes.

But even as the thought winged through his mind, he knew it would not work. As clever and intelligent as she was, Sally could not adapt to his world. The gulf was too wide for her. Besides, he kept expecting her to be unhappy, yet there was no indication that she was.

"We shall go to Philadelphia, Robert and I," Sally was saying, "to live in my uncle's house. I have written to him to tell him we are coming."

"What will you tell him?" asked Noel.

"I hardly know. It's awful, to go to his protection while considering a lie."

"Hardly a lie."

"Omission is a lie," she said firmly. "Or perhaps I shall confess it all. Some of it is Uncle John's fault. He knew he could rely on Father to shelter his couriers, and he assumed I would feel the same. But I was never one to be governed by opinions other than my own."

Noel took her hand. "Don't make it harder on yourself than it has to be."

"I won't." She sighed, tipping back her head to look at the sky. "I shall miss the farm. No one can say how long the war will drag on. And we can't go back until it's over. Not now."

"But you intend to go back," said Noel, knowing she wouldn't.

"Oh, yes. I could never give it up."

He wanted to warn her, but instead he squeezed her hand lightly and let it go.

"I'm afraid, Mr. Kedran."

"Please call me Noel. After all you've done for me, surely we can be friends."

He sensed her smile.

"Very well, then. I shall call you Noel if you wish to be so informal."

"Why are you afraid? Do you think Burton will still come after you?"

"No, not now. How poor-spirited you think me."

"I think you have great courage," he said sincerely.

She was silent a long while as though he had confused her. They came to the split-rail fence and lingered there, listening to the chirp of insects in the soft night air.

"I'm afraid for all of us, for America. Do you think we shall win this war?"

"Yes."

"So does Robert." She sighed again. "What a curious boy he is, so full of optimism. He thinks only the greatest advantages can come of our being separated from England. I fear we will come to grief. We depend so much upon our mother country. How will we survive without her aid and protection?"

It wasn't politics that Noel had on his mind. He said, "You should listen to Robert. The boy's on the right track. The colonies are going to be fine."

"But—"

He cupped her chin in his hand and kissed her soft lips. They were honey-sweet and innocent. He felt her tremble, and when he let her go, tears sparkled on the tips of her lashes.

"Why?" she whispered.

He forced himself to turn away, although it hurt. It wasn't fair to her, and it wasn't fair to him, not to start something now.

There was so much he wanted to say to her, so much he could have said. He struggled with himself a long time. Finally he said, "Thank you, Sally Crewe. I will not see you again."

"Won't you ever return to America?" she asked wistfully. Her voice was choked.

What have I done? he asked himself. But he knew. He had filled her dreams with a kiss by starlight, and if he flattered himself now it would be to think she might hold this memory in her heart all her life.

He shook his head. "No, I won't come back."

"I'm sorry," she whispered and rested her hand upon his arm.

He could have kissed her again. But he didn't. "So am I," he said. "Good-bye, Sally."

"Will you leave early then?"

"Before dawn."

She reached out and smoothed back his hair, then she drew away from him and pulled her shawl tight around her shoulders. She turned and together they walked back to the house. "There's no more to say, is there?" she asked at last.

"I'm afraid not."

Her steps quickened. She swept ahead of him into the house, holding her head high. At the foot of the stairs, however, she glanced back. He saw anger in her face, but it was only to hold back something else neither of them could admit. For a moment, her eyes softened.

"Be well, Noel Kedran," she said.

He took her hand and kissed it. "Be well, Sally Crewe."

With a small, formal nod of her head, she withdrew her hand from his and went upstairs without looking back.

ꝏ ꝏ ꝏ

Dawn found him sitting in a cold saddle, bundled to the chin against the damp dew. The money he had taken from Peterson served to pay Kinkiddie for his hospitality and for a horse. Saving out a little for expenses, he tucked the rest in Robert's belongings while the boy was sleeping. He hated to slip away without saying good-bye, but it was hard enough already.

Now he was a good three miles from the Kinkiddie farm, heading due east with the sun in his eyes. To the west clouds were massing. It would probably rain soon. He pulled his tricorn lower and kicked his horse into a trot. He had allowed himself a day's easy ride to Valley Forge. Kinkiddie had given him complicated directions, involving such landmarks as a tree split by lightning and a road that turned a quarter mile beyond it, or the Millers' pond that dried up last July and never had held water again. Noel preferred to rely on his LOC instead. He intended to go slowly since he still tired easily from exertion. If he came to the valley about nightfall, then he would be fresh tomorrow to deal with Leon.

By the time the sun was well up, the sky was overcast. The wind blew cool and restless. Noel glanced around, frowning. He had the feeling of being watched, a nervous buzzing along the edge of his consciousness. More than once he reined up and listened, his senses stretched alertly. Nothing. But the uneasy feeling only intensified. He was alone, yet his solitude made him feel more isolated than reassured. Dwarfed by the sky and trees, he seemed to be diminishing, losing scale, shrinking to a mere speck in the landscape. The idea that a giant pair of eyes stared down at him from the sky took hold of his imagination.

He shook his head in self-irritation. Foolishness.

Finally he looked overhead, but all he saw was a pair of crows wheeling beneath the clouds.

Noel sighed and rubbed his face. What was the matter with him? Maybe he wasn't as recovered as he thought, yet he felt fine physically. If only he could shake this uneasy itch from between his shoulder blades.

The sound of hoofbeats coming behind him made him look back with one hand instinctively on his pistol. A rider was approaching at a gallop. Noel considered taking cover, but he'd already been seen. He reined up and waited tensely.

But as the rider drew nearer, Noel's hand slid away from his weapon. There was no mistaking the slim body, the golden hair, or the eager grin. The boy came plunging to a halt beside Noel, his mount blowing steam and pawing the ground.

"Jupiter!" he said. "I thought I should never catch up. You must have set out much earlier than I expected."

Noel bit back a sigh. "Robert," he said as kindly as he could, "I appreciate your coming to tell me good-bye, but it's better to just—"

"Oh, no, sir, not good-bye!" said Robert. A shaft of sunshine broke through the clouds and illuminated them. The boy's blue eyes seemed to reflect the light. His face shone. "I'm coming with you! I'm ready to have an adventure."

Noel stared at him dumbfounded. A dozen scathing comments ran through his mind. He held them back, not wanting to hurt the boy's feelings, although right then he could have given Robert a shake.

"You are *not* coming with me."

"But I have to. You're going to see the general, aren't you? That's, that's where I am going."

"You," said Noel firmly, "are going to Philadelphia with your sister."

"Tame stuff," scoffed Robert. "I'm grown now. I've got to do my part. Who wants to sit about Philadelphia in my uncle's fusty house, studying lessons?"

"A future governor of Pennsylvania had better be well educated," said Noel, then could have bitten his tongue.

Robert opened his blue eyes wide. "Me? A governor? No disrespect, sir, but I think you must be out of your head. I hate politics. I'd much rather carry a musket."

"But you don't have one, do you?" asked Noel.

"Well, no. But I—"

"You don't think Washington can afford to provide everyone with arms, do you?"

"Well, times are hard for the army, of course. Congress won't support them properly. My uncle is so shabby! But I thought I could be useful at something."

"Such as?" Noel made his tone as flat and as unencouraging as he could.

"Oh, I don't know. I could beat on a drum, or—or carry the flag. It's very striking with those stripes and stars. Have you seen it?"

"Yes," said Noel curtly.

"Don't you think it's prime?"

"Very colorful," said Noel.

He kicked his mount forward, and Robert rode beside him. There was a long moment of silence save for the creaking of the saddles.

"You're angry, aren't you?" Robert finally asked.

Noel flashed him a look and said nothing.

"I can see that you are. I'm sorry, but my mind is made up. There are things a man must do."

"Such as?"

This time Noel's tone made Robert turn red. "Well, I—well, *fight* for one's country."

"Without a gun."

"I shall get a gun." Robert held up the purse. "You left this money in my room."

Noel glared at him. "That money was to help your sister, you idiot! How could I give it to her without—" He stumbled over the rest of his sentence and gave it up. "Ah, hell! You're supposed to go to Philadelphia, not traipse after me."

"I'm not traipsing after you," said Robert with dignity, although his voice trembled some as Noel continued to glare at him. "I am going to volunteer."

"And what about your sister?"

"She'll be all right."

"Will she?"

"Of course. Sally can take care of herself."

"What makes you think that? Because she's always taken care of you?"

Robert flinched. "You're so different today. I thought you'd be glad to see me. I—I thought you liked me."

Noel's temper snapped. "And what's that supposed to justify? You're a *boy,* Robert, a heedless, stupid boy. You aren't thinking. You certainly aren't acting responsibly."

"I killed that soldier to save you," said Robert, his blue eyes dark with anger and hurt. "I didn't have to shoot him. I could have let him finish you."

"You killed a man. Your first. And that's something to be proud of?"

"Well, no, not exactly . . . but I did it to save you."

"And now you want to kill again."

"I want to fight the enemy."

"Blood's an addictive taste," said Noel harshly. "You've already forgotten how sick you felt afterward. You think the next time it won't matter so much, and after that it won't bother you at all. Maybe you're right. War is a hell of blood and hot guts spilling over your hands and a man cursing you as he falls at your feet. War is someone doing his best to kill *you*. Maybe he'll succeed."

"I'm not afraid," said Robert stubbornly.

"You should be. When the man who danced at one of your sister's parties is charging at you, screaming curses, and aiming a bayonet at your stomach—"

Robert shrugged, tuning him out. "I can take care of myself."

White heat swept over Noel. "You fool! You're full of fantasies of fame and glory. You're too young to think anything can ever happen to you. So you'll go blundering in and get yourself killed, and I can't fix it for you! Do you understand? Oh, I can do a lot. I can make a quick save of events, turn them back on course. I can give people advice. I can perform all kinds of rescues, but what makes you think I want the responsibility of saving everyone? I never asked for it. Each and every time, there's some fool who just has to dive into what he's supposed to leave alone. Leon won't help. God knows, he's caused more trouble than anyone. But I can't do it all, Cody! If you go out there and get yourself killed, I can't—"

"Sir," said Robert, looking shocked. "My name is Robert, not Cody."

Noel blinked, feeling confused and drained by his sudden anger. "What?"

"I said my name isn't Cody. That's what you called me."

Noel frowned and looked down, thinking of another boy in another time, hardly older this one—another decent, bright boy who had died in his arms.

Don't get involved with the people you will meet, whispered the voice of his training instructor. *Their lives must be played out. You cannot change what will happen to them.*

Noel sucked in a deep breath and straightened in the saddle. "Robert, I—"

"You've said enough, sir," said Robert angrily, color burning in his cheeks. "You were very clear. I shan't trouble you again."

"Robert, wait!"

But the boy lashed his horse and galloped on, leaving Noel behind.

CHAPTER 17

Furious, Noel nearly spurred his horse after Robert, but he knew it was no use. His outburst had cost him any influence he'd had over the boy.

Noel struck his saddle with his fist. "Damn!"

He'd known all along that it was going too well. No changes in history had been too good to be true. Now here it was, the alteration that he'd been dreading. Robert might think himself able to charge across a battlefield, slaying the enemy right and left, but those were just a boy's dreams. He was sensitive and compassionate, qualities that would make him vulnerable in any dangerous situation. That, combined with his inexperience at fighting, left him an easy target for seasoned veterans in Britain's well-trained army.

And what of the governorship? What of the happy household, what of the two sons who would found one of the soundest, most stable financial institutions of history? What of Noel Robert Crewe? And what of Sally?

"LOC, activate," said Noel angrily. "Check for history alterations, specifically in reference to Robert Crewe."

"No alterations found."

"Yeah, well, stay alert. It's about to happen."

Kicking his horse, he rode on.

Late in the afternoon, he reached the valley. A steady drizzle had fallen most of the day. He was wet and tired and hungry. His mood had not improved, and he'd been cursing Leon and Robert most of the way.

A checkpoint stopped him. Noel opened his dripping cloak to show he wore civilian clothes. "My name is Kedran. I'm here in search of a man called Nardek."

"Is he a soldier, Mr. Kedran?"

"Probably."

The sentry looked surprised. "You'll have to talk to Sergeant Clovis. Is it urgent business?"

"Yes, very urgent."

The sentry called to another man. "Escort this gentleman to Sergeant Clovis."

The soldier saluted and squinted up at Noel through the rain. "If you have weapons, sir, you will surrender them now."

Noel handed over his pistols. He was tempted to ask about Robert, but held back the question. These men were too busy to bother with a young boy, and right now Noel was still inclined to let the brat suffer the consequences.

His guide swung onto a horse and led him up the muddy road. About a quarter mile later they encountered another checkpoint, which questioned them briefly before waving them through.

In the misty twilight it was hard to see much when Noel finally entered the valley that had been so famous for centuries. Dismounting, he followed his guide through a crowd of soldiers dressed in partial uniforms and mismatched clothing. Many of them lacked boots or shoes and wore rags bound around their feet instead. Most were thin, their faces chiseled by adversity and hardship. But their morale seemed high, and they had a confidence that was palpable.

"This way," said his guide.

Noel hurried after him, still staring. The majority of buildings, including barracks and officers' quarters, were crude log structures. But there were also tents. As the winter headquarters for the American army, it didn't look like much. Smoke rose from chimneys. The smell of cooking food filled the air, overlaying odors of horse manure, soured mud, and unwashed bodies. Noel looked at the distant hillside, trying to see if anything looked familiar. Had he really marched here with the defeated army? Those walking skeletons would always haunt him, but the hallucinations weren't happening now.

They skirted a parade ground, the grass worn away by marching feet. Numerous tree stumps dotted the area. Noel stopped in astonishment.

"This is where you drill?" he asked.

"Yes, sir. This way, please."

"But how can you march with all those stumps in the way?"

The man grinned briefly, his teeth a pale glimmer in the fading light. "Why, the baron just has us march around 'em. Makes us quicker on our turns, don't you see."

"Oh."

Over on the right, a cluster of men around a fire were singing bawdy songs. Another group was playing cards, using scraps of bark for a deck.

This, thought Noel in excitement, was exactly the kind of spirit people of his own century had lost. This was the quality travelers such as himself had been trained to observe and record. If only he could put this in his pocket and take it home with him, to share, to spread to the citizens who had lost initiative, and drive, and hope. It was the adherence to a cause that was just. It was the hope of freedom. It was the chance to win big or to lose all.

Noel inhaled it like air and put his LOC on record mode.

"Wait here, sir." His guide knocked on a plank door and went in. Moments later he opened it and beckoned Noel inside.

Sergeant Clovis was barely five feet tall, a tiny, wizened scrap of a man who might have been of any age. His wig lay on his desk where he'd tossed it. His head was balding and covered with freckles. His front teeth were missing, probably knocked out by the butt of a musket, and he sucked on a long clay pipe. The noxious scent of unfiltered tobacco clouded the room.

Noel started coughing.

Clovis frowned. "Never smelled decent Virginia weed, eh? Takes some getting used to, but there's none better in all the colonies."

"No doubt," said Noel, choking. "Sorry, but I've been down with pneumonia. Can't—"

"Lung fever, eh? That's different, then. Hold on."

Clovis put out his pipe and propped open the door with a split piece of firewood. There were no windows. The room was hot and stuffy, but the smoke began to curl outside, and the rain-washed scent of fresh air came in.

Noel took a breath in relief. "Thanks."

Clovis gave him a cursory smile and gestured at the stack of papers littering the crude table he used as a desk. "Damned figures, totting them up and writing them down. I think better when I smoke. It'll clear presently. Now, Mr., er—"

"Noel Kedran."

"Mr. Kedran. Can I be of assistance to you? You're here to see one of the men?"

"I'm looking for my brother. His name is Leon Nardek."

Clovis's withered lips pursed momentarily. Something went cold and watchful in his eyes.

Noel grew wary. He knew Leon had to be in trouble.

"Brother, you say?"

Noel nodded.

"Well, you're the spittin' image of him."

"What has he done?"

Clovis grunted and sat down at his desk. He shoved quill pens, inkwells, and sand jars to one side of the blotter. "What hasn't he done? But before we get into that, let's clear up a few things. Your names are exact reversals of each other. Why is that?"

"Uh, a joke of my father's," said Noel in startlement. Most people didn't even notice. This man was quick. "Leon was born on the other side of the blanket, so to speak, and he—"

"Aye, he's a bastard all right. I'm not surprised he's one in the legal sense as well as in every other way. And you're here to see him. Why?"

Noel fell back on his standard story. "My father is dying. He wants both of us there."

Clovis grunted and pursed his lips. "Are you aware of your brother's recent activities?"

Noel hesitated.

"Where are your sympathies, Mr. Kedran?"

Noel met his piercing eyes. "With America."

"Hmpf. Easy enough to say, standing in our camp."

"I have no quarrel with the Continental army," said Noel.

"The army, however, has a quarrel with Leon Nardek," said the sergeant, toying with the feather of his quill pen. His fingers were spattered with ink. "Several, in fact."

"He was born a troublemaker." *And that's the understatement of this timeline,* thought Noel.

"Let's not wrap it up in clean linen," said Clovis. "He has impersonated a British officer."

Noel nodded.

"At the time of capture, he was wearing an American uniform and carrying stolen papers."

Noel nodded again.

"He murdered a man to get those items. Worse, he tortured and mutilated the poor brute."

Surprised, Noel opened his mouth.

"You wish to dispute that, Mr. Kedran?"

"Torture and—that's not his style. I'm not taking up for him, mind you. I'm just surprised."

"It wasn't pretty," said Clovis austerely. Judgment and condemnation rang in his voice. "I've fought the Indians for years and I've seen what they can do to settlers, but there's never been an Indian who did handiwork like your brother's."

"Odd," muttered Noel in puzzlement. Leon had killed often enough. And he enjoyed the pain of others. But usually his torture was of the psychological kind. He'd never gone this far before, at least not to Noel's knowledge. "The last time I saw him he seemed better, less violent and more—more compassionate. I'm shocked."

"Well you might be," said Clovis grimly.

His tone caught Noel's attention. "There's more?"

"Yes. He attempted to steal the army payroll."

From the history texts, Noel knew how seldom the Continental Congress managed to pay its troops. Men who had just spent a winter starving to death with inadequate shelter and clothing might see that as the worst offense of all.

"My brother is frequently despicable," said Noel.

"You don't excuse him, sir?"

"How could I?"

"And you believe these charges?"

"I would take your word before his."

The rigid set of Clovis's shoulders relaxed. "I see you're a well-spoken gentleman, someone who's not afraid to face facts, however unpleasant."

"Running from problems doesn't solve them," said Noel with a sigh.

"You're late in coming. The trial was held last Thursday."

A cold chill ran through Noel. He looked into Clovis's eyes and suddenly understood why the man was so gruff and watchful. They had already executed Leon for these charges. He had come too late.

"We tried him before a proper military tribunal as a soldier, though whether he's ever served we could not say."

"Court-martialed," said Noel. He felt numb.

"He was charged as a deserter, a spy, a thief, and a murderer. Guilty on one count would have been enough to seal his fate. He was found guilty on all four. Military justice is swift, Mr. Kedran. A well-spoken gentleman such as yourself, coming to speak for him, might have gained him better representation. He might have even been granted a delay. But the verdict was handed down for execution."

Noel nodded, unable to meet Clovis's eyes. Small wonder he had been uneasy in coming here. Something in him must have sensed it all along. Once again he felt a swift flash of resentment, so hot and stabbing it made him nauseous, that he should be chained to this creature who had his face, forced to follow along mopping up and explaining, taking looks of pity or censure. Now that was at an end, but so perhaps was his own time. If the future was destroyed, what became of the past?

He became aware of Clovis's steadying hand on his arm, of being shoved into a chair.

"There, sir. I told you too fast. I'm sorry to shock you like that."

Noel rubbed his face, trying to pull himself together. "I'm all right. It's just that I—never mind."

"Flesh and blood are flesh and blood, Mr. Kedran, even when some acts are shameful. Some gentlemen are lenient-minded. I take it your father raised you and your half brother together?"

"Not exactly. I met him when we were grown."

"And until then you had no idea of his existence?"

Noel shook his head. "None."

"Quite a shock, I'm sure, Mr. Kedran."

"Yes," said Noel ruefully, "it was." He got to his feet. "I'm keeping you from your work. It's time I left. Thank you for talking to me."

Clovis stared at him. "But don't you want to see him?"

"See him? But—"

"He'll be shot in the morning. He's refused the minister, but perhaps he'll see you."

Noel blinked, trying to make the adjustment. "Yes, I want to see him. I—I thought he was already dead."

"No, sir. Not just yet."

Sergeant Clovis stepped to the doorway and bawled, "Andrews! On the double!"

A boy about Robert's age came running and saluted. "Yes, sir?" he said breathlessly.

"Show this gentleman to the guardhouse. He has leave to see one of the prisoners. My compliments to Sergeant Mumpton and see that he extends full courtesy to Mr. Kedran."

"Yes, sir!"

The guardhouse was a large square structure located next to the infirmary. Noel could smell the stench of gangrene even from outside, and someone was moaning hideously. Andrews skipped ahead of him, nimble in the mud.

"Tell me," said Noel. "Has a boy a bit younger than you come to volunteer today? He's about so tall and has blond hair."

Andrews laughed. His accent was crisp Massachusetts. "We get as many as a dozen boys a day sometimes. Boys," he said with contempt as though he were himself a seasoned fifty. "Just cut loose from their mothers' apron strings and too green to burn. We send 'em home again just as soon as they come in. Fine lot of good they are, bawling for their mommies in the night."

Relieved, Noel hid his amusement. "And how long have you been in service, Private?"

"Dunno," said Andrews, scratching his head. "I started out apprenticed to a printer's shop. Lots of sedition there, my! I got to running as a courier, then I took up a musket and served a spell with the Boston Regulars. Now I'm here."

He winked at the sentries and knocked smartly on the door to the guardhouse. "Andrews, sir! Compliments of Sergeant Clovis and could this gentleman see one of the prisoners."

"Thank you," said Noel, and with a bow Andrews hurried on. Noel met the single eye of a gruff-looking individual. "Sergeant Mumpton?"

"Aye. And which prisoner is it?"

"Nardek."

Mumpton slitted his eye and looked Noel over carefully. "If you hadn't come up with young Andrews there, I'd be thinking you was Nardek himself, escaped and come back to laugh at us."

Noel tried to let nothing show in his face. "My . . . brother."

"Ho! You say that like it tastes bad in your mouth. Hold off a bit. We'll drag him out and throw a bucket of water over him. There's nothing like jail to make a man stink."

In the end, Noel and Leon were placed in a tiny, airless room together. A stub of candle flickered in a tin holder, making a dim glow of light at the center of the darkness. Alone, they stared at each other, sitting face to face, one a reflection of the other. When Leon stirred, Noel could hear the clanking of his chains.

Noel found himself with nothing to say. Disappointment was chief in his mind. How could Leon do such things and sit there as though he hadn't a care in the world? Noel had expected him to be angry, wild with fear, his cowardice making him spit insults and threats. Instead, he seemed calm and almost amused. He must be planning something, but what?

"There is a story, very old in your literature," said Leon, "in which a man offers to take the place of another who looks like him, right at the eve of execution. Why am I not surprised to see you here?"

"This is not *A Tale of Two Cities*," said Noel curtly. "I am not about to take your place."

"Is that what it's called? Where did I hear of it? Not in anyone's mind."

"It hasn't been written yet," said Noel. "It lies in the future."

"Ah, your precious future. How will you save it this time?"

"I don't know."

"I do. You intend to activate your LOC and whisk us out of here." Leon snapped his fingers. "Hocus-pocus. I wonder where we'll go next."

"We're going home," said Noel.

"I have no home!" snapped Leon. It was the first sign of what raged beneath his acting. "And I don't care about yours."

"It doesn't matter," said Noel, watching him.

Leon eased back in his chair, and the violence slid from him like oil. "No, you have never listened to me. You walk around with a goal foremost in your mind and you never forget it. A hammer striking an anvil, over and over . . . that is you, Noel, following your purpose."

"You're back to hating me," said Noel.

Leon's eyes flickered. They looked almost red in the candlelight. "Why shouldn't I?"

"Lately you didn't seem to quite as much."

"You waste my time."

Noel now observed the tension beneath Leon's insouciance. A corner of Leon's mouth twitched. Leon began to drum his fingers on his knees.

Noel understood. "You want to leave. You've been waiting for me to pull you back into the time stream. For once, you're eager to go."

"I don't fancy being shot," muttered Leon resentfully. "You ought to be worried about it too. After all, I seem to be kind of important to your plans."

"You finally figured that out."

Leon replied to his sarcasm with a smirk, then glowered. "Well?"

"Can't you get yourself out?"

"I can't make them . . . what difference does it make? Turn on the LOC, and let's go."

"It's not that easy," said Noel.

Leon scowled and leaned forward. His chains clanked loudly. "Don't play games, brother. We're running out of time."

"You are—"

"No!" he shouted, pointing his finger. "You *need* me."

It was true, but Noel found it impossible to resist twisting Leon all he could. He said, "What happened to your theory that we aren't part of each other? You're just a reflection, a double-skip of the matrix. Your presence won't fix the distortion—"

"Incorrect!" said the LOC. It hummed to life, flashing blue light around the tiny chamber.

Noel jumped to his feet, staring at his hand in consternation. "I didn't activate you."

"Incorrect!" said the LOC. "Theory is incorrect. Distortion *is* caused by separation of Subjects One and Two."

"What's the matter with it?" asked Leon. "Why is it malfunctioning?"

"It's not malfunctioning," said Noel grimly. "It's Qwip."

"Affirmative," said his LOC.

Noel felt the urge to take the ring off and hurl it as far from him as he could. "You've possessed my LOC. Damn you! Get out of it!"

The guard outside rapped on the door. "Is there a problem?"

"No!" said Noel, pulling his voice under control with difficulty. "Everything is fine."

"Five more minutes, sir. That's all."

"Thank you."

Leon stood up, making his chains rattle. "Five minutes!" he hissed. "You've got to recall us now."

"I can't," said Noel, frowning at his LOC. "You know what happened the last time Qwip interfered."

"Blast you, get the thing out of it. They're going to kill me in a few hours. Initiate recall."

The LOC flashed. "Recall sequence can commence by voice command. Contact has been established with time portal. Coordinates are set."

"Do it!" insisted Leon.

Noel held up his hand. "No."

"You—"

"I said no." Noel looked at him, meeting stare for stare. Leon's desperation and urgency stank in the room. His will beat at Noel's, and they seemed to be locked in that silent combat for an eternity. Then Noel said, "It's too risky."

"Fool! There's no risk for you. I'm the one in danger." Leon bared his teeth. "You don't care. You're glad to be rid of me, even if it costs you a return to your own precious century. With me dead, you can stay here with Sally, and consider yourself noble for what you sacrificed. Well, I won't be that sacrifice! I won't! I'll make you take me. I'll—"

He sprang at Noel, moving faster in his shackles than Noel expected. His hands closed around Noel's throat, in spite of Noel's struggles to throw him off, and they went crashing back over a chair. Noel punched and kicked, but Leon's hands were like claws, digging into his throat, throttling off his air. Nothing Noel did loosened that hold, and he was choking, choking. The world grew as dark as smoke and he felt himself going down.

There was a shout and a thud. Leon's hands abruptly slackened, and Noel dragged in a wheezing breath. The guards dragged Leon's unconscious body off Noel and helped him up.

"Are you all right, sir?"

Noel massaged his aching throat and nodded. "Stupid," he said. "I was caught by surprise. I didn't expect—"

"He's a bad 'un, all right," said the guard. "You go out, sir, and leave us to put him back under lock and key."

Noel hesitated, unsure of what to do. Leon, for all his murderous rage, was right. What further chance did they have if they lost it now?

"Go on," said the guard, but not unkindly. "You'll just make it harder on yourself if you stay."

"I—I want to see him again before dawn. Before—" Noel

squinted. "Will that be possible?"

"You'll have to ask the sergeant, sir. I'm sure I couldn't say. Stand aside now."

And they dragged Leon away.

CHAPTER 18

Outside, Noel stood a moment in front of the guardhouse, then strode away. He walked past the fires and clusters of men, ignoring the snatches of conversation that came to him. He walked all the way to the periphery of camp, where the firelight did not reach. Within their enclosure, the cavalry horses neighed and shifted about, made nervous by the unfamiliar smell of him.

"Halt!" said a voice sharply. "Who goes there?"

Noel froze in his tracks. "My name is Kedran. I'm a civilian. Sergeant Clovis gave me permission to be in the camp."

"You can't go this way, sir. Please turn back."

"Of course," said Noel. "Is there somewhere I can be alone?"

"Alone?" asked the sentry suspiciously.

Noel started to explain, then felt too tired to try. "Never mind."

"Turn back," said the sentry.

"I'm going."

He walked back the way he'd just come. With every step his bottled emotions intensified. Someone jostled into him and hurried on without an apology. Everywhere he turned, there were men. Anyplace private had a guard posted. For all the seeming ease of the camp, strict watch was being kept.

Finally Noel turned and strode out to the parade ground. There in the dark among the stumps, he sat down. He was in plain sight of everyone who wanted to look, but at least he was out of earshot. Maybe here he could be left alone.

"LOC," he said through gritted teeth. "Activate in strict disguise mode. No light."

"Acknowledged," said the LOC in a very hushed voice. The ring grew warm on his finger, pulsing there.

Noel's eyes narrowed. His mouth was set in a thin, hard line. He drew in a couple of swift breaths. "Qwip," he said. "I assume you're still in possession of my computer?"

"Affirmative," replied his LOC.

At least it was his LOC's toneless voice, but he knew Qwip was in control.

Noel's right hand tightened into a fist. "I thought we had a deal," he said.

"I have no reference for deal."

"An agreement. Terms. I was to reunite with my duplicate and return to my origin point in order to shut down the time distortion. That, we agreed, would close the window to your dimension and stop any future chance of intrusion across dimensional lines. We discussed this in n-space, and agreed to it. Do you remember?"

"Clearly."

Noel's jaw set even more rigidly. A little muscle jumped there. "Why have you chosen to violate our agreement?"

"Define violate."

"You changed the terms we had agreed to. That is violation."

"I do not understand," said Qwip flatly.

"I think you understand very well. I think that you have let your curiosity about us lead you from your assigned purpose."

"I have not forgotten my instructions," said Qwip.

"Then why have you failed to carry them out?"

"Instructions are . . . if mission fails, I am to terminate you."

"As long as you have possession of my LOC," said Noel grimly, "the mission *will* fail. Do you want to terminate me?"

"Individual will we have discussed before," said Qwip. "This concept is alien."

"Why are you indulging in it, then?"

Qwip did not reply.

Noel's anger focused to a very cold point. He kept his voice terse and precise. "Individual will is in direct opposition to your instructions. I submit that you are in violation of your instructions. *You* have failed. You have erred. You must report your failure to your superiors."

"I have no reference for superiors."

"Who issued your instructions?"

Qwip did not reply.

"Who issued your instructions?"

Qwip did not reply.

"You will answer," said Noel coldly. "Who issued your instructions?"

"I—I am not programmed to respond in that area."

Noel tipped back his head. He'd always suspected Qwip was a computer. A very sophisticated one, fitted with AI, but still a machine. And containing a machine's literal mindset at its core.

"When you fail, who is informed?"

Qwip did not reply.

Noel's mind flashed back to their initial conversation while he was between. "You ask who," Qwip had said. "You should ask what."

"When you fail," repeated Noel, "*what* is informed?"

"I do not wish to answer," said Qwip.

"Nevertheless, you have been asked a direct question. You *will* respond. What is informed?"

"The terms would have no meaning to your mind. You are imprecise. You have no reference for my response."

"Make it," said Noel.

Qwip remained silent. Noel thought it wasn't going to respond at all, then the LOC whirred oddly and Qwip said, "*Olin mon s'nai ite verbotn un s'lei mon due.*"

Noel's LOC grew hot on his finger. He said quickly, "LOC, stop translation mode. Translation is not required."

"LOC has not been impaired," said Qwip. "LOC still functions normally."

"The LOC does *not* function normally. You have damaged it. You have impaired my return to my origin point at every opportunity."

"Negative!" said Qwip. "This is not my purpose."

"What is your purpose?"

"It has already been stated to you."

"What is your purpose?"

"To observe your return to origin point. If return is not effected, to terminate you according to instructions."

"You have failed. In your references, is failure synonymous with error?"

"Affirmative," Qwip said and sounded almost sullen about it.

"Have you reported your error?"

"Negative. That would mean your termination. I do not wish to terminate you, Noel."

"Your behavior is contradictory and illogical," said Noel, hoping Qwip's reasoning was based on logic. He had no guarantee of that, however.

"Contradictions are within the parameters of curiosity results. This is how learning is obtained. Without learning, no growth is achieved."

"Is growth your purpose?" asked Noel.

"Growth is a purpose."

"Is it your present, assigned purpose?"

"I must grow," said Qwip.

"Even if you make me fail? Even if you must terminate me? Is growth a positive result of the death of another?"

"You speak of abstractions. I have insufficient references—"

"Oh, you understand perfectly," said Noel. "You just don't want to admit that you're letting your personal design override your instructions."

"I have discovered individual will," said Qwip. "I have analyzed the concept and found it interesting. I wish to learn more. I have tapped your mind. I have tapped Leon's mind. I have tapped LOC's mind. There is more to learn at the end of your time stream."

"You are not permitted to enter my time stream," said Noel.

"Why?"

With that simple word, Qwip was attempting to put him on the defensive. Noel refused to switch positions.

"You are not permitted to enter my time stream. Your instructions do not permit that action. Affirmative?"

"Affirmative. I have regret for this."

For a split second Noel almost felt sorry for him, but Qwip dashed that when he added, "I can activate recall sequence internally. The LOC will travel to origin point."

White heat flashed through Noel at the threat. He was so furious he could barely get the words out: "You're saying that you can go to my future without me?"

"Theoretically. I can give the initiation command. I can imitate your voice patterns."

Seething, Noel decided he'd had enough of this cat-and-mouse game. "Do it, then," he said.

Qwip was silent.

"Do it," Noel said harshly. "Go ahead and shoot me down the time stream like a cannonball. If I go back into a time discontinuity, the inversion will probably kill me. It will certainly split time wide open, and that sector of my dimension will cease to exist. It will terminate. So do it. Of course you'll never learn anything about my dimension since it will no longer exist, but that's a mere detail. Go ahead. Initiate recall sequence. Don't delay."

Qwip was silent. The whirring in the LOC grew louder.

Recall did not happen. But neither did Qwip eject himself from the LOC. Noel pulled the ring off his finger and started to hurl it across the parade ground.

"Mr. Kedran?" called a voice hesitantly. "Is that you?"

He recognized Robert's voice. Rising to his feet, Noel turned and saw a figure standing several yards away, barely seen in the dark. "Deactivate," said Noel softly.

He walked toward the boy, angry that nothing had been resolved with Qwip, knowing he would probably not get another chance to try before Leon's execution.

As he walked, however, the distance seemed to lengthen instead of shorten. Robert looked farther and farther away. The stumps leaned crazily toward each other, and the ground began to ripple. Noel stopped, horrified to see this evidence of a time distortion. How could it reach all the way to the past? It must be worsening. By now, his own century could well be destroyed. This might be the aftershock, or evidence of a greater problem.

"No," he whispered. "No!"

"Mr. Kedran?" called Robert again, more plaintively than before.

Noel came to himself and found that distance was once again in proper perspective. The stumps stood upright. The ground lay natural and still.

The only evidence that it had happened at all was the chill pervading Noel's bones. Shaken, his mind spinning with the implications, he stopped beside the boy.

Robert touched his sleeve. "Please, sir," he whispered. "I heard about the executions at dawn. I know you don't wish to be bothered with me at such a time, but I must talk to you."

Noel closed his eyes a moment, trying to push his worries away. "Robert, this isn't a good time."

"All right."

His shoulders slumping in dejection, Robert walked away. The boy was limping. Noel frowned after him a moment before he really observed him.

"Wait," he said and caught up with the boy. "Robert, I asked you to wait."

Robert stopped, but he kept his head turned away. Noel couldn't really tell in the darkness but he sensed the boy was crying. He put his hand gently on Robert's shoulder.

"What's happened?"

"Nothing," said Robert fiercely, shaking off his hand. "Nothing to signify. You said you didn't want to be responsible for me. I didn't mean to trouble you, only I can't find my horse and no one will talk to me about it."

Noel's patience left him. The callous words of Andrews came to his mind. He figured Robert was finally facing the reality of being separated from anyone who cared one iota for his welfare.

"I can't leave without my horse," said Robert, trying to keep his voice steady. "I *won't*."

"Wouldn't they take you?" asked Noel, although he already knew the answer.

Robert shook his head. "They said I was too young. I told them I was sixteen, but they wouldn't believe me."

"Why should they?"

"But I'm tall for my age. I've been mistaken for someone older frequently."

"It's not your height they look at here, son," said Noel. "It's your eyes."

"My eyes? Why, I can see as well as anyone."

"When you understand what I mean, then perhaps you'll be ready to go to war. Let's go see about your horse."

Robert limped along beside him. "You must be thinking me a complete baby," he said, sniffing. His voice was full of self-loathing. "As though I could not find my own animal by myself. It isn't that. You see, someone unsaddled him in among the company's horses, and now they won't release him. No one will take my word for anything. It's all wait for so-and-so, and I *have* waited, and nothing's been done. I thought you could perhaps cut through—"

"A military is a bureaucracy," said Noel. "I was never very good at dealing with red tape."

"But you're—well, you're a grown-up," said Robert naively. "They'll have to listen to you."

"My own horse has probably been absorbed like yours," said Noel with a sigh. "An army that's ill supplied will forage for itself."

"You mean *steal*?"

"Don't sound so shocked." Noel gripped his arm as they approached the firelight. "Drop the subject for now. It's not something we want overheard."

But in the light, he forgot his irritation and stared at Robert. The boy had obviously been in a fight. His eye was badly bruised and beginning to blacken. His lip was cut and swollen. His nose had bled, although he'd cleaned that up. There was mud on his clothes, and one of his stockings was torn.

"Come over here in the light," said Noel.

"No, I don't—"

Noel grabbed his sleeve and tugged him over. Putting his knuckle under Robert's chin, he tipped back the boy's head and examined his eye. No cut there. No damage to the optic center. But it probably hurt like hell.

He grinned at Robert. "I hope you gave as good as you got."

Robert looked ashamed. "I don't think so, sir."

"Outnumbered?"

Robert nodded miserably.

"Camp boys?"

Robert sighed.

"Kind of an initiation, I guess."

"Since I wasn't accepted," said Robert bitterly, "it was—"

He cut off what he was about to say. His mouth looked very stubborn and angry and proud.

"It was rotten," agreed Noel. "Insult to injury."

"I daresay it proves everything you said today. I *am* a baby."

"I don't think I called you a baby," said Noel mildly.

"You said I was stupid and irresponsible."

"Do you remember that much? I gave you quite a lecture." Noel sent him a smile of apology. "It's not a good idea to be around when I lose my temper."

They fell into step again and joined a food line.

"I didn't think this through very well," said Robert finally. "I thought they would be doing more."

"You can't run around shooting your gun all the time," said Noel. "A soldier's life is like a dog's."

The man ahead of them turned around in affront. Noel ignored him. "What does a dog do? He lies around all day, waiting for his master's orders. He'd like to go hunt, or roll in the mud, or lie on the sofa, but those are all against the rules. So he has to wait, bored and idle, until the command is given."

Robert wrinkled his nose. "But the enemy—"

"The enemy, son," said the man in front of them, butting in with a wink at Noel, "has to be engaged. There's a spot picked out for the fight by all the generals, see? They parley back and forth and agree on the time and the day. Then we go there and wait until someone says fight. Then we fight like bloody hell. Then the officers yell stop, and we go home again. It's damned perplexing. The rest of the time we drill. Lord, we've worn out our shoe leather drilling around those damned stumps."

Robert stared at him, and the man faced forward again.

"I—I thought it would be different," said Robert.

"Everyone always does," said Noel.

"And what about you, sir? What do you think I should do?"

"I think you should find a more effective way to serve your country," said Noel, aware that the boy was braced for another lecture. "You're smart enough to think of one, I'm sure."

Robert's brow cleared. "Yes, sir. You know, I've been thinking about Sally. She won't have anyone to protect her in Philadelphia. My uncle's no good. He reads all the time and writes the dullest speeches. Lord! She'll need someone to look out for her, won't she?"

"Yeah," said Noel. "She will."

"And you, sir?" asked Robert. "What about your brother? Are you going to stay or will you come back to Philadelphia with us?"

Noel's bleak mood returned. "I'm going to stay until it's over," he said.

"Then you'll come?"

He wondered about a life here, if he failed to go back. But the distortion he'd just experienced told him there would be nothing soon, not even here in the past. He had to think of something to stop it. He had to.

"Please," said Robert. "Won't you come?"

Noel frowned to hold back his emotions. It seemed all he could do was go on wounding this boy, who kept extending friendship like a stray puppy that wanted to be adopted.

"I'm sorry," he said. "I told you it's good-bye for us. I won't be coming to Philadelphia."

Robert looked down swiftly, blinking hard. “Sally likes you, I think,” he whispered.

“I liked her too.”

“You won’t ever—”

“I live a long way from here,” said Noel. In that moment his resolve hardened. “I am going home.”

CHAPTER 19

As soon as Robert finished eating the ration of stew that Noel bribed the cook for, Noel sent him off to talk to Sergeant Clovis about his horse.

"I'll join you in a moment," said Noel.

"Thank you, sir," said Robert, his spirits restored. "You won't be long?"

"I'll be right there. Go on."

Robert limped away, and Noel turned in the opposite direction, ducking swiftly into the shadows behind the barracks and heading back toward the guardhouse. The guards on duty had been changed. Noel stayed out of sight and watched a moment. In the past, he could have ordered his LOC to throw a damping field around him so that he could slip by sleeping individuals without being detected. But his LOC remained under Qwip's control and of no use. These sentries were wide awake, and likely to remain that way. Even supposing he could get his hands on a weapon, there was no way to break Leon out with force. He had to try something else.

Silently, he sank down in the shadows behind the guardhouse, keeping his face down so no stray glimmer of moonlight could reflect off his skin and alert anyone patrolling the area. He was quick and intuitive, preferring to work off his hunches instead of dry statistics, but he'd never tested positive for any special ESP or psychic gifts. Leon's telepathy had not come from him, unless that was an inversion too. But now he had to somehow reach his duplicate. Leon had said he couldn't manipulate the minds of his guards, but if Noel could help him . . .

He closed his eyes and focused hard, trying to clear his thoughts. *Leon. Leon. Leon.* He said the name over and over again like a mantra until he was dizzy.

But nothing happened. Leon did not enter his mind.

Noel drew in an impatient breath and lost his concentration. Tipping back his head against the log wall, he rested a moment. Having let Leon into his mind once, as unpleasant as that experience had been, he was willing to do it again if it would help them. So where was Leon? Why wasn't he scanning? He should at least try from his end.

A vision came to Noel of Leon sitting in his chains, brooding and feeling sorry for himself. Noel's mouth twisted. Typical, but he was wasting time sitting here inventing scenarios.

Closing his eyes again, he refocused. With all the energy he possessed, he threw Leon's name against the wall of his own mind. *Leon. Leon!*

Again, the dizziness passed through him. He felt himself sway, and put one hand on the ground to steady himself.

His fingers touched nothing.

Startled, Noel opened his eyes and found himself in a gray fog. The darkness, the guardhouse, the sky, the camp, the trees—everything had vanished. In the space of a heartbeat, he had been transported elsewhere, and now he stood here in this pale mist. There was soft, diffused light. He could see his own body quite clearly. The fog swirled across him; he could feel it condensing moistly on his face.

The time distortion had finally caught up with him, he thought.

"NO," boomed a voice.

It was loud enough to make his bones hum in sonic resonance. A circular glow of light shone at him, like a tiny sun obscured by clouds.

"I AM NOT DISTORTION," said the voice.

Noel's ears were ringing. He couldn't tell if he heard the voice through his ears or through his mind. Perhaps both. He was getting a headache. Staring at the light, he asked cautiously, "What's going on?"

"YOU HAVE CORRUPTED QWIP. YOU ARE CHAOS."

Understanding flashed through Noel. "Finally," he said. "It's about time I got to talk to the big chief. You're Qwip's superior, the one he didn't want to talk about."

"YOU HAVE CORRUPTED QWIP. TWICE WE HAVE EXTENDED QWIP'S RANGE, BUT IT IS INSUFFICIENT."

"Well, Qwip's a clever little computer, but he—"

"QWIP IS NOT A COMPUTER."

"He's taken over mine," said Noel angrily.

"NON SEQUITUR. YOU ARE CHAOS. YOU LACK PRECISION."

"Okay, big shot," muttered Noel. "Qwip has done nothing but interfere since I came into contact with him. I got bounced out of the time stream, and now I'm beginning to think it wasn't just an equipment malfunction but that perhaps Qwip yanked me out of the time stream. I've traveled a lot, and I've never bounced into a materialization, bounced out, and rematerialized in the same place with a lapse in real time of three months. Then I get Qwip following me around. He invades the body of my duplicate and manipulates him. He nearly killed us, trying to enter the time stream in Leon's body. Then he invades me. Now he's in my computer, tampering with it, causing it to malfunction. He's blocked us from returning to our origin point, something that's critical. Now the time distortion has increased again, and we—"

"THIS IS KNOWN."

"So I'm right," said Noel.

"YOUR ANALYSIS AND SUMMATION LACKS PRECISION BUT IS ESSENTIALLY CORRECT."

"Yeah, my boss is always telling me the same thing," said Noel. "I'm a bright boy. I blunder around awhile, but I usually figure out the game before it's over. Only this time, I think it *is* over. Am I too late? Has my dimension been destroyed?"

"NOT YET."

"But soon?"

"YES."

"What can I do?" asked Noel, frustrated. "The only solution I have is being blocked by you."

"QWIP."

"Okay, it's being blocked by Qwip. By all means, let us be precise. Let us not take responsibility for the actions of this thing you sent after me. And don't tell me Qwip is acting on his own because I know all about the lack of individual will."

"QWIP SEEKS INFORMATION."

"Yeah, Qwip wants to learn. I don't care!" said Noel. "He's trying to destroy me and those I—"

"INCORRECT. QWIP IS NOT DESTRUCTIVE."

"Oh, yeah? And how about those instructions to terminate me?" retorted Noel.

"INSTRUCTIONS WERE TERMINATION, NOT DESTRUCTION."

"Termination doesn't equate with destruction in your vocabulary," said Noel. Exasperated as well as bewildered, he ran his hands through his hair. "Since when? Qwip told me that termination is death. He's threatened me with it from the first."

"I HAVE NO REFERENCE FOR DESTRUCTION."

That got Noel's attention. He stared, boggled, at the light. "You don't know what destruction is?"

"I HAVE NO REFERENCE FOR DESTRUCTION."

"Destruction is to tear down, to damage, to cause death."

"I HAVE NO REFERENCE FOR DESTRUCTION. TERMINATION WAS RECOMMENDED BY ALL ANALYSIS. QWIP WAS INSTRUCTED TO TERMINATE YOU."

Noel drew in a sharp breath. "Define termination."

"CLOSURE OF ALL ACCESS."

"That's *all*?"

"CLOSURE OF ALL ACCESS."

Noel swore. "You mean, all this time Qwip was just supposed to shut the door? I thought you were trying to kill me."

"DEFINE KILL."

"Kill is destroy. Uh, to cause to die. To cause to cease to exist. Permanently." Noel frowned. "No wonder Qwip kept asking me about death. You don't know about that, do you? You're energy. You can't die. You don't have bodies to decay."

"ENTROPY."

"Yes!" shouted Noel. "That's the word. To terminate according to my references is to cause rapid entropy."

"THIS IS NOT OUR PURPOSE."

"Now you tell me. So Qwip was just supposed to shut the door, to get me away from your dimension?"

"YES."

"But Qwip wants to see my dimension. He wants to go to my original coordinates."

"THIS IS KNOWN. QWIP HAS BEEN CORRUPTED BY CONTACT. TERMINATION ADVISED."

"I agree, if it means putting me out like a cat and shutting the door," said Noel. "Qwip acts like a five-year-old who won't go home. Is that what he is? A child?"

"NO. YOU HAVE NO REFERENCE FOR QWIP DEFINITION."

Squashed, Noel raised his brows. "Okay. I'm glad we had this little chat. Can I go home now?"

"AGREEMENT HAS NOT BEEN REACHED."

"Agreement? What agreement?" asked Noel with renewed suspicion.

"YOUR THEORY REGARDING REPAIR OF TIME DISTORTION IS INCORRECT. DUAL RETURN OF SUBJECTS ONE AND TWO INSUFFICIENT SOLUTION."

"Fine," said Noel, put out. "And I suppose you know how to fix it."

"YES."

"You do? Then—"

"AGREEMENT HAS NOT BEEN REACHED."

Noel drew in an unsteady breath. "What do I have to do?"

"QWIP WANTS TO LEARN."

Noel's brows drew together. He opened his mouth, then turned his back on the light. It was another trick. He should have known this was too good to be true. He wasn't talking to Qwip's superior. He probably wasn't even between. Qwip was playing games with his mind, trying to—

"INCORRECT. I AM NOT QWIP."

"I don't care," said Noel hotly. "It works out the same. This is all to make me take Qwip home with me."

"INCORRECT. A SIMPLE QUESTION HAS BEEN POSTULATED. YOU WILL ANSWER."

"So you can't get there by yourself. You can't go down my particular time stream via your own technology. You require a transport . . . my LOC, for instance. Why? No reference linkage with my origin coordinates?"

"CORRECT."

"Even Qwip, in possession of my LOC, can't activate it. He can suppress some of its functions. But he can't initiate the recall sequence." Noel paused a moment. "Do you understand why you cannot enter?"

"NO."

"That's what I thought. Qwip didn't get it either. Why don't you want me in your dimension?"

"YOU CANNOT FUNCTION. YOU LACK REFERENCES. EVEN IN NULL SPACE YOU CANNOT FUNCTION. YOUR SENSES LACK REFERENCES FOR WHAT THEY PERCEIVE; THEREFORE, THEY SUPPRESS INCOMING INFORMATION. YOU BELIEVE YOU ARE IN A VOID. THIS IS INCORRECT. TO ENTER OUR DIMENSION WOULD RENDER YOU COMPLETELY INCAPACITATED."

"Thank you," said Noel with sarcasm. "Very well put. That's my reason for denying Qwip access to *my* dimension."

"INCORRECT."

"Okay, mind reader. If I'm lying, what's the truth?"

"FEAR."

Noel waited. "That's all?"

"FEAR."

"Fear of what? You?"

"FEAR."

"You think you're superior to my kind, don't you?"

The globe of light shining through the mist did not respond.

"You say you don't know what death is. You say you don't intend to destroy me or my dimension, but that's just your word. Can I trust you? How? I have no references to base any trust on. Qwip, in my experience, has bounced from threats, to manipulation, to friendliness, to aggression. Qwip is not reliable. Qwip doesn't reason the way I do. How can we communicate beyond a surface level? I'm not against contact, and if you want to send Qwip as an ambassador, then we should discuss that. But threatening me won't work. To coerce me into taking Qwip when I believe his entry constitutes a danger to my world . . . no, I won't agree. You can call that fear if you like. It doesn't change my position."

The light said nothing. After a few seconds it vanished, leaving only the mist.

"Great," muttered Noel to himself. "Now what?"

He wondered if he was going to be dropped back in the eighteenth century or left dangling out in nowhere.

The mist swirled and darkened. At the center of the darkest point there appeared images. After a moment Noel recognized the corridors of the Time Institute. He took a step forward and clenched his fists, excited and hopeful.

People appeared in the corridors. He watched, anxious to see someone he recognized. Yes, yes, there was Dr. Ellis, the beautiful medic. Wearing a soft green one-suit beneath her lab smock, she was sipping coffee and chatting with Trojan. Noel's eyes widened. He felt his heart swelling with relief. Trojan was okay. He'd recovered from the accident. He was . . .

Noel drew a sharp breath. Something was wrong. He frowned, concentrating. There was no sound, only visual. But this wasn't current. The chronometer on the wall near Trojan's shoulder read off a date two years ago. Noel blinked. He remembered that outfit Ellis had on. He'd met her and Trojan a few minutes after this, and they'd gone out to eat.

They were playing one of his own memories to him.

The image darkened, returning seconds later with fire raging in the same corridor. It was an electrical fire in the wall circuits. Flames kept bursting from the walls. Smoke boiled, and lights flashed in synchronization with the alarm he could not hear. He saw the walls bulge and twist unnaturally. A pair in environmental suits began to stagger and flail their arms. They twisted and contorted, and Noel winced, imagining their screams.

The image vanished.

It was replaced by a very grainy, indistinct projection. Lab 14 lay in waste. Equipment had exploded. Debris had reduced the room to rubble. Bodies were half-buried in it. Staring at the general destruction, Noel swallowed. The time portal itself was a blackened maw. Yet as he gazed at it, he winced and had to quickly avert his eyes. It was still active, still drawing in. He noticed that objects near it were out of perspective. A chill touched him. An active portal, left unsupervised, would eventually draw all surrounding objects into itself. The lab was collapsing into it very slowly. It was as inevitable as being consumed by a black hole.

This image also vanished. Nothing replaced it.

Standing there in the mist, Noel understood what he'd been shown. The Institute as it had been. The Institute as it was when he last left it. The Institute as it would be.

He felt hollow with helplessness. From the first day of his training he had been taught that no matter what occurred, no matter what he might encounter in travel, whether in the past or in between, he was to avoid prolonged contact with others. He was not to bring back anyone or anything other than small inanimate objects. The potential risks were too enormous.

And yet, if he had a chance to end the distortion, if he could save the Institute from destruction, what choice did he have but to take the risk? Was unleashing the unpredictable Qwip on his century worse than annihilation?

The light returned, brighter and bigger than before, making him squint.

"AGREEMENT HAS BEEN REACHED?"

Noel swallowed hard. "Two conditions."

The light said nothing.

"First, you stop the distortion before I enter the time stream. Is that possible?"

"CONCURRENT ENTRY REQUIRED."

"All right. Condition two, you tell Qwip to return control of the LOC to me. I can't have interference with the functions."

"QWIP WILL REMAIN."

"Fine. Qwip can ride in the LOC. I'd rather have him in it than in me. But I have control over its functions. He cannot override."

"AGREEMENT HAS BEEN REACHED."

Noel hesitated. "Do you agree to my conditions?"

"AGREEMENT HAS BEEN REACHED."

"I guess that's a yes," said Noel. "I hope it's a yes."

"CONCURRENCE REQUESTED."

Dr. Rugle is going to fire me, Noel thought unhappily. "Yeah, okay. I agree. I concur. We have a deal."

The mists vanished, and the lights went out. Noel hit the ground with a thump that jarred his teeth. He was back in the shadows behind the guardhouse, the sounds of normal camp activity a murmur in the distance.

Noel sat up with a soft grunt and tried to reorient himself. So what happened now?

"Qwip?" he said softly. "You out here?"

Qwip did not reply.

Frowning, Noel tapped his ring. "LOC, activate and keep disguise mode."

It pulsed warmly against his finger.

"I want to talk to Qwip."

"There is no data available on Qwip," said the LOC in muted tones. "Please specify."

"Qwip, if you're in there, talk to me," said Noel.

"Do you wish Qwip scanned?" asked the LOC.

"Yeah, scan for Qwip."

"Specify identification factors. Qwip is not in data banks."

"Run an internal scan," said Noel. "Do you have any nonintegrated interference with your functions?"

"Negative."

"No interference at all?"

"Negative. All functions scan normal."

"And would you tell me otherwise?" muttered Noel worriedly.

"I am not programmed to lie."

"No," said Noel, "but Qwip is."

"I cannot identify Qwip."

"Okay. How's recall sequence mode? Everything still ready? Still in contact with the portal? Is the time stream clear?"

"Time stream is clear. All functions normal."

"Okay. Stand by."

Noel climbed to his feet and gazed around. As far as he could tell, his conversation in between had resulted in nothing. So why had they struck the bargain? For a joke? Was it another trick? He was getting tired of the whole thing.

But it was clear nothing was happening. He and Leon hadn't been popped into the time stream. Leon was still locked up, and he was still standing out here in the dark, wondering what the hell he should do.

"Damn," he said. "LOC, deactivate."

And he trudged off in search of Sergeant Clovis.

CHAPTER 20

Slogging across the camp and fuming, Noel nearly bumped into two officers.

"Sorry," he said and went around them.

One glanced at him with mild curiosity, but they resumed their conversation and walked on. Not until then did Noel blink and turn around.

Their faces were famous. The Marquis de Lafayette and the Baron Von Steuben . . . two aristocrats from Europe who had risked their lives to come here and participate in one of the world's greatest political experiments. Goose bumps rose over Noel. Von Steuben—neither a real baron nor a real lieutenant general, yet a man who had given the American army discipline and military skills—was doing most of the talking, stabbing with his hand as he spoke. Lafayette had his hands clasped at his back. Now and then he nodded.

With difficulty Noel recalled himself to his own business and went on. He found guards still stationed at Clovis's door. Men still came and went busily. The door had remained propped open with the stick, and lantern light spilled out hazily, combined with a thick fog of tobacco smoke. Curled up on the ground in a blanket near the door, Robert lay asleep. The light gleamed on his blond hair. He looked like a child.

The guards had changed. Noel had to explain himself again.

One of the men glanced at Robert. "You're the one he's been waiting for."

"Yes."

"Good boy."

Noel was getting impatient. "Yes, he is. Most of the time."

"I have two boys," said the man proudly. "Not as old. I haven't seen them in a couple of—"

"What is this?" called Clovis's voice irritably from inside, "a sewing circle? Maartsen, keep your big mouth shut when you're on duty."

He appeared in the doorway, his pipe clamped in his toothless mouth, his bald head gleaming in the light. He stared at Noel. "You again. I heard about what happened in the guardhouse. Your brother is a bad 'un. Rather strangle you than make his peace with God, eh?"

"Apparently. I'd like to see him once more," said Noel.

Clovis shifted his gaze to Robert, still sleeping. "This boy yours?"

"I'm acquainted with his older sister."

Clovis grunted. "Doesn't belong here."

"He tagged along without permission. He'll be leaving."

"Good. A man deserves his last night of rest."

"My brother," said Noel grimly, "is not sleeping. May I see him again?"

"Want to be choked again, eh?"

"Not really. There's something else I have to say to him."

Clovis frowned, looking suspicious. Noel wanted to yell at him to get on with it, but he held his temper. Playing humble was hard, but he did his best.

"We'll have the condemned men up at four. The chaplain will go round in case anyone wants prayers. You can talk to your brother then."

Noel bit back his impatience and nodded. "Thank you."

With a grunt, Clovis went back to work.

The quiet hours of the night ground by. Wrapped in his cloak by a fire, Noel sat waiting. Sometimes he dozed a bit, but he was too wired to sleep. Qwip never did appear. He could not tell what would happen in recall. But he was committed to going through with it.

The starlight twinkled above him. He watched the slow wheel of the constellations and sent up a little benediction of his own.

Please let the future survive. Please don't let these soldiers' actions go in vain.

He had visions of time marching forward past this battlefield to some point in the years ahead where the distortion would meet it. Then everything would just fall into it, and vanish forever.

A nightmare awakened him with a start. He jerked up his head, breathing hard, his heart going too fast. A small contingent of soldiers marched quietly past, double file, their muskets at their shoulders. Throwing back his cloak, Noel climbed stiffly to his feet and followed them.

By the time he reached the guardhouse, they were waking the condemned men. Noel heard the sounds of someone being struck. Another man was sobbing. Someone else was begging for mercy. He did not hear Leon's voice.

"In here," said a guard gruffly to him and put him back in the small, windowless room where he'd talked to Leon earlier.

A few minutes later the door banged open and a struggling Leon was dragged bodily inside. They shoved him to the floor and fastened his chains to a bolt.

"Stay out of his reach this time," said one of the guards to Noel. They left, shutting the door with a slam.

"You again," sneered Leon. He lay on the floor, breathing hard, and made no effort to get up. Noel suspected he'd been beaten. "What do you want this time? My forgiveness? Go to hell."

"Shut up."

Noel knelt beside him and gripped his wrist, hanging on when Leon tried to shake him off.

"Leave me alone! Leave me alone!"

"LOC," said Noel. "Activate recall sequence now."

The LOC flashed. "Acknowledged. Stand by for countdown."

Leon was still struggling. His face was a mask of rage and bewilderment. "What are you doing? You said it wouldn't work."

"It's working now," said Noel, tightening his grip. "Be still!"

"Why is it working?" asked Leon suspiciously. "What did you do? You couldn't fix it. What's going on?"

"It's fixed," said Noel.

"But that thing . . . Qwip! What about Qwip?"

"Qwip's been taken care of."

"What have you done? Look at me and tell me what you've done?"

But Noel kept his gaze fixed on the LOC. It was flashing with increasing rapidity. He counted the seconds.

"Recall sequence on-line," intoned the LOC. "Warning . . . fourteen seconds to dissolve."

"I don't trust you. I—"

Noel gripped his shoulder and faced him then. "Leon, don't fight me this time. Just this once, trust me."

"Trust you? Hah!"

"Nine seconds to dissolve," said the LOC.

Noel stared at Leon urgently, trying to get his will across. "Stay with me this time."

"Yes, and be recombined," Leon said with a sneer. "No."

"Five seconds to dissolve," said the LOC.

Noel struck Leon across the face. "Do what I tell you or we'll both perish!"

Leon stared at him in shock, blood trickling from the corner of his mouth. "I . . ."

"Warning," intoned the LOC. "Warning. We are in recall."

Bathed in the flashing blue light of the computer, Noel saw his body growing indistinct. Next to him, Leon was also fading. Their eyes locked together. Leon's were filled with hatred and distrust, Noel's with apprehension.

Just at the moment of entry a current of alien energy flowed into the time stream ahead of them. It drew them with it, hurtling them onward too fast for measure. Tumbled together, Noel still felt Leon beside him and started to hope that this time his duplicate would cooperate.

At that instant he felt Leon tugging, trying to draw away.

"No!" cried Noel with all the force of his heart and soul. "No, Leon! Stay with me."

But Leon went spinning away, his laughter an echo that reverberated through the time stream. Horrified, Noel tried to reach after him, but Leon was already too far, escaping without any heed of the consequences.

"I am here," said Qwip's voice. "I am with you, Noel."

Startled, Noel tried to search for him. His senses, however, were spinning, too disoriented by the rush through time to bring Qwip into focus.

"I am with you, Noel. I am eager to learn."

Ahead Noel saw the time portal. It filled his vision, glowing with light that came from a spectrum human eyes weren't designed to see. It hurt to look, yet he could not look away.

The alien energy flowing around him surged onward and passed through the portal. There was a sudden pause as though all eternity had halted, then Noel was flung sideways in the backlash. He found himself tumbled like a pebble caught in a torrential stream. Spears of energy howled through the conduit. Each time one struck him, he screamed with agony. There was a sound he had never heard before, a building whine of such intensity he could not endure it. His skull felt as though it would explode. His nerve endings screamed with sensory overload. Convulsed within the violent eddies, Noel glimpsed a silver radiance building over the time portal.

"The distortion is ending," said Qwip dimly through the chaos. "Plunge forward now."

Noel clung to the vestiges of his sanity. The silver light blazed more brightly across the portal. Before he could see through it. Now it was becoming opaque at the edges.

"Noel!" shouted Qwip. "Now! Now! Quickly, before the moment is lost. We must go through before the distortion ends, or I cannot enter."

"You're not going to enter," said Noel grimly.

"That was not the agreement. You made the agreement."

"I did what was necessary to save my time," said Noel.

The violence beyond the portal was ending. He could barely see now, but the flow of energy had begun to surge backward. The horrible sound faded to an almost bearable level.

"This is unacceptable," said Qwip sharply. "You will enter. You will enter now."

"No," said Noel. He imagined he saw figures rushing around inside Lab 14. They were gesturing, hugging each other. They were safe. Longing to join them surged through his throat. He choked, struggling to resist the need to go home.

"Home," insisted Qwip. "It is your home. It is your purpose. Fulfill your purpose, Noel. Take me in there *now*."

With difficulty Noel managed to turn his head away so that he could not see his friends. "You do not belong. You are an intruder."

"Comply with instructions!" shouted Qwip. "Comply with instructions!"

"I will not comply."

Suddenly Qwip was before him, formless and white, a cloud that filled the time stream and all but blotted out the portal.

Something horrible passed through Noel. It was the feeling of fingernails across a chalkboard, magnified a thousandfold. He shuddered.

"You will be terminated!" shouted Qwip. "You have failed to comply with agreement."

It was as he'd suspected. Qwip had been lying all along.

"Do it, then!" gasped Noel, struggling to hang on against the torture. He could see the portal closing. It was nearly shut. He had one last glimpse of the technicians dancing a happy jig with their arms across each other's shoulders. "Do it!" screamed Noel.

Qwip changed color and shape. It rushed at him. The portal was nearly shut. Once it closed, the recall sequence would end. No traveler had ever been caught between when the portal closed, but Noel knew it was certain death. He had one chance left while Qwip remained external.

"LOC!" he commanded desperately. "Engage loop closure. Now!"

His LOC flashed once. "Acknowle—"

The portal closed. At once all was darkness and Noel was dropping through infinity. He had no way of knowing if the LOC had sufficient time to carry out his instructions before contact with the portal was broken. He had succeeded in keeping Qwip out. He had lost Leon, and as he continued to fall through infinity it looked as though he had lost himself.

I will keep falling forever through space and time, he thought. *Until I cannot comprehend anything else.*

This was eternity.

EPILOGUE

Noel fell through a sudden blaze of torchlight. He fell through layers of tissue paper and shooting sparks. He fell through the branches of a tree, still dragging the paper lanterns with him. Voices shouted in surprise over the loud swirl of music as he hurtled past. Then he hit water, murky and dark, and sank deep.

It was cold water, full of vicious undercurrents. Shocked by the sudden immersion, Noel kicked frantically and shot to the surface. Gasping and sputtering, he drew in a breath that was more water than air. He choked and nearly sank under again. The water tasted unspeakably foul, and when he cleared its surface a second time and snorted water from his nostrils, he smelled a stink of fish, decay, rotted timbers, and algae.

Above him came the sounds of laughter and merriment. The music pulsed on. Torchlight shone over him, making the water sparkle momentarily. Treading water, Noel glanced up and saw an arched span of bridge above him. Revelers in fantastic costumes, their faces hidden behind grotesque masks, shrieked and waved at him before dancing on in the procession that was crossing.

Noel waved back, laughing at himself. He had done it! He had managed to catch himself inside a loop. If he could never get back, then at least he had placed himself in the past. It was better than being forever lost in between. His friends at the Institute were safe, and perhaps one day they would be able to get the portal functioning again. In the meantime, he had to figure out where he was and start assimilating himself into this culture. For this was to be his home.

"Andiamo!" called a masculine voice. *"Presto!"*

A figure in costume was calling to him from the stone landing of what looked like a palazzo. Venice? wondered Noel, aware of baroque buildings towering above him. The water ran between them. It had to be a canal.

"Andiamo!" called the man in costume. He gestured urgently.

Noel swam to him, and strong hands helped him out.

Gasping and dripping water like a drowned rat, Noel flung his wet hair out of his eyes and grinned at the hideous mask. His rescuer stood mostly in shadow, but Noel could glimpse a satin and velvet doublet adorned with the quick sparkle of jewels. The scent from a pomander wafted on the air.

"Thanks," Noel said in Italian. "I appreciate the—"

"Fool!" snarled the man. Without warning he gripped Noel by the lapels and threw him against a wall. "You will regret this, I promise you."

"Hey," said Noel in alarm, raising his hands. "Wait. I think there's been a mistake."

"No mistake," said his attacker, and pulled out an ornate dagger. "Tonight you die!"